VICIOUS LITTLE MONKEYS

Kenneth J. McKay

Cover Art by Jaclyn McKay

www.jaclynmckaydesign.com

Copyright © 2012 Kenneth J. McKay

NE CEDE MALIS BOOKS

necedemalisbooks@gmail.com

ISBN: 0615785018
ISBN-13: 978-0615785011

For Camille,
Forever.

CONTENTS

	Foreword	3
1	High and Mighty	5
2	College Boy	29
3	Remnants	57
4	Scarecrow	77
5	Prima	111
6	Boar's Head	137

.

FOREWORD

This is a collective novel about the people of a shared place, a place that shaped their lives and their souls, and as such, it subscribes to no particular plot device, nor should it. It can be vulgar, violent, profane and ugly; yet graceful, fragile, profound and beautiful - much as life itself.

This is a work of fiction...

We think we understand each other, but we never really do.
-    Luigi Pirandello

HIGH AND MIGHTY

The sun yearned over his shoulder like an anxious outsider, casting long shadows across his path in a desperate cry for attention, but to no avail. He walked on, treading without notice or care upon the forlorn silhouettes on the sidewalk before him. The sun might have once been lord of the day, but it had no such imperious presence now. It was either there or it wasn't, merely a bystander to the day's events. The Bronx was a practical parent. The mother-borough would never let her children become beguiled by any such capricious fancies as sunrises and sunsets. This wasn't a disheartening reflection of the way things were, no lack of poetry in the lives of the people; it was just a fact. He had somewhere to be whether the sun was there or not.

He walked on.

The sun accepted his indifference and resigned itself to lonely solace above the streets of Van Nest. The brave, yet rusting neighborhood fenced in by the Bronx River Parkway and the train tracks that cut a trough alongside East Tremont Avenue was like a funnel that poured into the South Bronx. Not so much a border town as it was the smeared edge of a cultural spectacle. Blacks, Hispanics and stray whites were smudged together in the few square city blocks between West Farms and the predominantly white middle-class gateway of Morris Park to the east and north. Coexistence in this urban buffer zone held its own.

He moved with experience through the streets, each footstep retracing the thousands made before, but his journey was his own. Motion didn't propel him, purpose did.

Mike was an Everyman with a twist. Having lived all of his nearly thirty years on the same street and coming through them somewhat in tact was what set him apart from many of his contemporaries. He had cruised through his teens a popular local, moving easily into post high school with a steady job as a construction laborer by day and a part-time college student at night. He was as comfortable on a cement stoop or park bench as he was behind a desk in the Fordham University library. He had the gift of fitting in anywhere and with anyone. He could just as easily churn out a distasteful joke over a lunch time beer with his fellow construction workers as debate a point of conflict with his professors.

Though he treasured his childhood of curbs, stoops, park benches, and street corners, he knew that he would some day have to move on. The neighborhood that had been his playground as a boy could just as easily become his battleground as a man. He knew that there would have to be a cut-off point, and that time had come. The streets of his youth belonged in the fond memories of childhood, not in the sad futures of unfulfilled manhood. He had seen all this early on and had prepared for it. Having worked his way through school, he was finally done, and now he was ready to make his move and nothing would turn him away from his purpose.

He walked on.

Mike had a ten o'clock interview at Argus and Williams, Inc., New York City's second largest construction firm, only this time he was looking to move up from the work site to the front office. He was armed with an MBA in business management and ten years of experience in the trenches. He would move up off of the streets and into the sky. It wasn't a power trip; it was the call of wonder. Watching a city grow and change was like seeing creation itself, a re-evolving and renewing Genesis. The living city. He wanted to be a greater part of it.

He walked along with a pure heart, but not an entirely clear head. The streets don't let go so easily of their own, and he was not without burden. But, for now, that was in the back of his mind. Once he got past this interview, he could find a way to deal with it. Just keep moving, he told himself.

Keep moving.

He was so intent on getting to the subway station that he was walking in a near blindness. He didn't see the other man until he was almost upon him.

Shit! Fucking Danny. I need him right now like a hole in the head. Maybe he didn't see me yet. Just keep moving.

It was too late – the other man caught sight of Mike just as Mike saw him.

"Hey, Mikey," came the slow drawl.

Fuck!

Mike's instinct was to keep moving, but his heart brought him to a stop. Though he lived just five blocks from the East 180th Street Station, he had given himself plenty of time to spare this morning, just in case. Danny was one of those cases. He had known Danny all his life and he couldn't just sweep past him. Mike had a soft spot for all the neighborhood losers. He somehow saw the good in each of them. It wasn't their fault, he told himself. Mike knew how cruel the streets could be, how they gripped some people and never let them go. Danny was one of the left-behinds, one of those that would never break free. Just like someone else.

Back of the mind, back of the mind.

Mike stopped.

Just give him a second. He never has much to say.

"Hey, man. You got a cigarette?" came the inevitable words from Danny's lips. It was the universal street greeting.

"Nah, Danny. I don't smoke," he answered as he had thousands of times over the years. Mike had never smoked a day in his life, but Danny's mind was long gone and Mike forgave him every time. He was used to it. Anger was not only wasted on Danny, it was somewhat unfair. The guy was just a victim. Just like someone else.

Back of the mind.

Danny sniffed the eternal sniffle of someone whose nose has been so eaten away by cocaine and whatever else could be snorted that it can no longer contain itself. His hair hung from his head like dead worms and his hands flitted nervously like they were trying to shake off a drip. He was still on some kind of residual high.

A hard partying night, hey Danny?

He was a sad case but Mike never looked down on him for it. Just like…back of the mind. I don't have time for this shit today.

"Hey, you think you could lend me twenty until later?" came the expected follow through.

"Nah, Danny. Not today. Look, man. I gotta' go. All right? Maybe I'll see you later."

"Yeah, okay," Danny responded, not the least bit affected by coming up dry on Mike. Mike was right. Danny didn't even realize what he was saying half the time. The requests were automatic. They were just a form of survival for the hopeless. If they ever reaped anything then it was just a lucky day, if not, then no harm done. Danny's hand raised slightly in a makeshift wave. As weak as it was, it was the sincerest form of gratitude he could muster.

Mike scooted past Danny and focused once more on getting to the train. He still had plenty of time to get downtown and be at least an hour early for his interview. Danny hadn't been much of an obstacle in his course. He didn't like having to blow him off, but he had a purpose today.

Danny was behind him now, and he could hear the trains rumbling across the elevated tracks just a few blocks away. Then, somewhere in between the sound of the trains and the smacking of his own feet on the sidewalk, Danny's voice sliced through his mind.

"Hey, tell David I'll see him later."

It's funny how the things that you so neatly tuck away in the back of your mind come slamming forward when you least expect them, or can handle them.

Mike's heart stopped before his feet did. He turned back to see Danny already meandering away down the street. *Did he really say that? Was I just imagining it? No, couldn't have been. He said something else. Keep moving.*

Mike started moving again, but not in the direction he expected. Not in the direction he should have been moving. Where the elevated subway tracks and the East 180th Street station should have been looming in front of him, all he saw was Danny's retreating figure now getting closer.

"Danny. Hey, Danny!" he heard his voice calling out. *What am I doing? I've got to get out of here. This guy is still half whacked. He couldn't have known what he was saying.*

"Danny!" he called louder, finally reaching the drooping figure and grasping his shoulder. Danny flinched out of instinct, like a startled animal. He obviously hadn't heard Mike's beckoning through his own haze.

"Hey, man! Oh… Mike. Hey, you scared the shit out of me. You could have given me a heart attack or something," said Danny, now cracking a half-smile. "Damn. You got a cigarette, man. My hands are shaking."

"Sorry, Danny," said Mike. "I just thought I heard you say something about David. Did you go see him upstate or something?"

Mike knew no one visited David. At this point, visitors were discouraged. After walking out of three rehab centers in the city in the past two years, David had been placed in a more extreme program upstate. The judge had ordered it after David failed to meet the requirements of his sentence.

The courts were lenient on drug offenders that at least pretended to follow rehab recommendations, but David had managed to piss off a liberal judge and four social workers. He was in last chance status. His next step would be a vacation in Riker's.

He's got to be mistaken.

"No, man. Not upstate," came Danny's slow and muddled reply.

Mike's neck tensed as the sound of the approaching #2 train echoed off the walls of the buildings around him. He should have been on that train. *Damn it!* At this time of day they come every ten minutes. He still had time, but Danny was wasting it. His patience was thinning.

"Danny, David is upstate. How are you going to see him later? When did you see him?"

Danny was too slow on the uptake now. Mike grabbed him by the shoulders and pulled him up straight.

"Danny. When did you see David?"

"Last night, man. I saw him last night," Danny's voice had somehow responded to Mike's escalating urgency. The slight smile was gone, replaced by confusion. He tried to shrug off Mike's grip but Mike had drifted into a haze of his own.

He stared at Danny for a second after his reply, but it wasn't Danny's face that he saw. It was David's.

Last night.

He didn't question it. It just sunk down into his belly like he had swallowed a stone. As much as he wanted Danny to be wrong, for all this to be some screwed-up, time-warped flashback from a drug-addled mind, he could feel that it was real. With David, all the nightmares were real.

Last night.

Mike's grip on Danny tightened even more. "Where, Danny! Where did you see him?"

Danny's face seemed to regain some form of vitality as Mike tasked his faculties. The deeply buried remnants of a viable mind stirred in his head. His eyes pulled in tight as he fought to focus his thoughts. It wasn't remembering the events of the night before that challenged him - it was understanding their correlation to the current situation.

"Uh," came first. "Uh…over on Hunt Avenue. I was going to Dean's and David was kinda' walking around, you know. He said he just came back from that shit-hole upstate, man. I said, 'Come on to Dean's', but he said he would catch me later. I figured I'd just see him at Twenty-Seven."

Twenty-Seven!

The stone in Mike's belly grew to a boulder

"Twenty-Seven" was the neighborhood name for the roof of the Bronxdale Apartments; a large apartment complex built in the early Seventies about a half-mile to the north. Its solitary central tower stood at twenty-six stories and was the highest point for miles around. An urban Everest. Originally meant to be a somewhat exclusive apartment building, it gradually became nothing more than a mirror image of the housing projects of Castle Hill. A column of low-income housing shooting straight up into the sky.

The Bronxdale Apartments' rooftop, with its aerie-like viewpoint, had inevitably become a "because it's there" destination. Kids would come from blocks around just to glimpse the streets that they lived and played on from a different perspective; try to find their own houses in the panorama, or just to hang out. There was exhilaration in the vertigo of staring down at your life. An out-of-body experience without ever leaving your body. The rooftop became an attraction, but not always an innocent one.

Nighttime on Twenty-Seven was owned by dopers and dealers. From their point high above the world, they could see cops coming for a half-mile around, and with two stairwells leading down from the roof, they could easily avoid anybody on their way up. No matter how many times the building superintendent tried to secure the rooftop doors, somehow they always managed to get busted open.

He eventually gave up out of fear and frustration and just started calling the cops, who quickly tired of the constant trips up the elevator and the climb up the roof stairs. They only went up now when things started flying off the roof.

Mike had been up to Twenty-Seven a lot of times as a young kid. It was where he got his first glimpse out across the city. He could see out over most of Van Nest, Morris Park, as far south as West Farms, and almost to the fringes of Parkchester. He could even see the Manhattan skyline in the distance. It was where Mike found his destiny, staring out across the city. It was also where his brother found his.

Where Mike would go up to Twenty-Seven to look for his future, David would go there to hide from it.

Even though David was older by two years, Mike was the older brother in every real way. Mike was always the one looking after David. He had the scars to prove it - inside and out. The only thing Mike couldn't protect his brother from was himself. David was always a wiry kid with an unfocused energy - a dangerous quality on the Bronx streets. Though he never really hurt anyone but himself, David had a reputation as "wild".

Drugs found David at an early age. His first hit from a joint was a pass-through while sitting in between Jackie Hagan and Loco Freddy on one of the park benches surrounding the tiny Van Nest Park over in the Five Corners – a desperate oasis of trees and asphalt that held a small city-style playground. By sixteen, reefer was no longer enough for him. He moved up from the park benches to the rooftop of Twenty-Seven. Hash, THC, speed – they were the staples of the world above the streets, and David wasted no time embracing them. As his teen years waned, David's old favorites gave way to cocaine and the early run of crack in the eighties. Minor busts quickly accompanied his new interests. Mike had retrieved his brother from nearly every Precinct between West Farms and Throggs Neck. It wasn't long before he was past due on IOUs from every cop, cop's brother, cousin, or friend he knew. Finally, after the well had run dry on favors for David, and his run-ins with the cops mounted, the courts attempted to do what Mike never could - force David into rehab. It was a weight off his shoulders, but not off his heart. He hated seeing his brother like that, but he was at the end of his rope. This last time, the judge ordered David into a program that was a combination of rehab and incarceration. Mike had hoped it would work, at least for a while, but he had a buried feeling that it would never, or could never, work for David. That thought had finally gnawed its way into reality.

Mike loosed his hold on Danny and the man collapsed into his normal slouch. He fidgeted for a second; uncomfortable in his awareness that Mike was upset about David. Awareness is the bogey man for people like Danny and David. It's what sends them running to Twenty-Seven. Some people can't handle what the world is made of, how it operates, so they find their own way to deal with things, or not.

"That place was no good for David," Danny responded in defense, a feat greater than Mike could realize. "They were trying to fuck him up in there, man. All these people telling him what's wrong with him. They were trying to…" he didn't get his chance to finish.

Mike grasped Danny again by the collar and pulled his face close. "They were trying to help him, Danny. Help him, you asshole. Keep him out of fucking jail! Keep him alive! When are you fucking guys going to realize that people are trying to help you! You walk around in a haze, pissing your lives against the wall, never thinking that maybe you're not only wasting your lives, but sucking the life out of others too. Look at you, man! You wander around bumming smokes and copping dope. How fucking long do you think you can live like that? Huh, Danny? How long? HOW LONG CAN MY BROTHER LIVE LIKE THAT!"

Danny squirmed within Mike's grip like a fearful child in an angry drunk's clutches. The sight made Mike feel ashamed. It wasn't Danny's fault that the world could sometimes be a lousy place.

"Shit, he said softly, releasing Danny, and hating everything that had happened in the past ten minutes. He should have just kept walking.

Danny stepped back quickly, but didn't move to leave. He just stood there watching Mike for a moment, then he spoke in as resolute a voice as he was capable of.

"David belongs here, man. Not in some shitty rehab with a bunch of scumbags picking him apart. You should know that, Mike. Don't let them turn you, man. Don't get high and mighty like them - judging people and looking down on them. David is good people. He belongs here. This is his home."

Mike's eyes met Danny's. It was almost bizarre to have someone as seemingly detached as Danny making declarations about "home". Until that moment, he had never considered that Danny, or even David, held any such equity in anything but their own addictions. In that moment, he was drawn into his brother's world and felt something that he had never thought about before - the tenuous sense of family that existed between people like Danny and David. Where Mike was David's brother by blood, Danny was a brother by ceremony. A brother, a family, a home.

His home? His home.

The boulder in Mike's gut had erupted into his head. A loud, messy blowout of brains, blood, and memories was seconds away.

Mike turned away from Danny and without a word started moving again. His feet retraced their steps back to where they were before he was derailed by Danny and found their path back toward the station. Danny called out something as Mike left, but the rumble of the trains was the only thing Mike could hear now.

Not now. I don't need this now. He couldn't wait one more day before pulling this on me. One day. Not even a day, just a few hours. I can't deal with this now. He's going to have to wait. Let him stay up on Twenty-Seven, he's better off there. Better off "at home". Or maybe he'll jump and finally cut me loose.

Mike stopped in his tracks with this thought. "No, David. I'm sorry," he said aloud, as if his brother might have heard him. "It's just that I …not today. Damn it! Not today."

Mike walked on. He reached the East 180th Street Station with just enough time to get on the next #2 train and get downtown. He pulled one of the five tokens he had brought with him - extras just in case - deposited one in the slot and pushed his way through the turnstile. He bounded up the stairs that led to the platform and positioned himself right where he knew the train doors would open. Less than two minutes passed before the distinct sound of an approaching train began to rumble across the platform. He could feel the vibration beneath his feet.

Not today, David. Not today.

The train roared into the station, the metal-on-metal screeching of the wheels on the tracks cut through the ears of potential riders like an old siren. The train came to a gradual stop and the doors slid open with a loud clank. The muffled voice of the conductor called out in a loud, but barely audible belch, "East 180th, #2 Express. Next stop East Tremont." Mike was right in front of the doors of the middle car as they opened. They weren't merely the doors of an old subway car. Today, they were the doors of opportunity for him. They would carry him toward his future.

Not today, David. Back of the mind.

After a minute, the sound of the conductor called out again. "Watch the closing doors. East Tremont, next stop." The doors closed and the train moved out of the station, taking its rumble with it until the platform was silent and empty once again.

He took the long platform stairs in leaps and emerged from the station in a heedless stride. The East 180th Street Station was behind him now. He could hear the distant sound of the #2 heading for its next stop. A stop he wouldn't see. The scorned sun pressed down hard upon him now, no more silent pleading. Its harsh light scattered any shadows and licked his neck, but he walked on. He had somewhere to be whether the sun was there or not.

He lifted his eyes above the streets and sought his new destination. He knew right where it would be. Sticking up into the sky in the distance ahead of him like a weary headstone was the tall gray column of the Bronxdale Apartments.

He walked on.

Time was unusually cruel to Mike on this late morning. Just barely an hour ago, he thought he had plenty to spare, but then in an instant came Danny… and David; and the world hit the brakes. It seemed as if it had taken him hours to walk the mile or so from the subway station to the unseemly building of dirty concrete and dull windows. The old routine of pushing a random apartment bell at the laughable security entrance and announcing "UPS man" took five tries before someone bought the ruse, though Mike believed that after all these years, the tenants just buzzed everyone in instead of dealing with the constant bell ringing. Even the damn elevator dragged itself toward the top floor. When the doors finally opened, Mike burst from them and bounded up the short flight of stairs to the roof door, glad to be free of the stifling air in the creaking shoe box. He hesitated at the door. He wasn't sure if he was ready for what was behind it. He took a deep breath and pushed the door open.

The rooftop of Twenty-Seven was empty. He stepped from the shadow of the open door, wedging it with the brick that was always left there for this purpose, and moved across the broad surface of crumbled asphalt that coated the wide roof, his feet making a familiar crunching sound that he hadn't heard in years. Mike hadn't been up on this roof for a long time, maybe ten years, but he knew it as if he were there yesterday.

He could tell right away that he was alone.

"David," he called. Nothing answered but a dull breeze.

He could see the city skyline rising on all sides of him and his frustration began to rise anew. He should be halfway into Manhattan by now, not up on some roof.

"DAVID," he shouted. "DAVID, WHERE THE FUCK ARE YOU?"

There was no one there.

Mike let loose a roar that would either release the pounding boulder in his head or pull his balls up and out of his mouth. As both of these outcomes seemed closer to reality, a voice cut above his own.

"HEY!" came the man's call. "You get your ass of this roof. I'm tired of you crackheads and assholes coming up here all the time. People are trying to live here; we don't need you up here." The man was clearly agitated. His pronounced Spanish accent was strengthened by his own anger.

"I'm looking for somebody," Mike said.

The man was fuming. "Who are you looking for on a fucking roof! Get out of here now." The man kicked the brick away from the door.

Mike's frustration was tempered by the man's appearance and the growing threat of an altercation.

"Okay, okay," Mike said with his hands out in front of him in a display of acquiescence. He took one last look around for any sign of his brother. There was none.

Jesus, David. Now what?

As he approached the man, Mike asked, "Did you see anybody up here last night or today?"

"No," answered the man flatly. "Now get the fuck off my roof."

Mike brushed past the man without another glance and headed down the stairs. He heard the door being pulled tightly shut behind them.

"Don't you come back here no more," called the man at Mike's back. "You don't belong here. You or your piece of shit friends."

The man's presence on the roof may have cooled Mike's outward anger, but he was still a knot of fire and chaos and though he may not have had the right to trespass, he nonetheless had the need; and the referral to his brother as a "piece of shit" was closer to a fatal mistake than the man realized. Mike stopped on the stairs and turned back to face him.

"Who the FUCK are you talking to!" said Mike, his fist clenching by his side.

"Come on," said the smaller man, pushing out his chest like a bird puffing its feathers to seem more menacing. "I ain't afraid of you."

"I don't give a shit what you're afraid of," Mike countered, his fist opening just enough to allow a sharply pointed finger to escape and move toward the man's face, "but don't make the mistake of assuming you know what's going on, so BACK DOWN, ASSHOLE. Lock up your fucking roof and SHUT THE FUCK UP BEFORE I TOSS YOUR ASS OFF OF IT!"

Something in Mike's tone reached the man and he said no more.

Mike turned back to the stairs and headed down. As he made his way down, his apprehension came up to meet him. *Where can he be? Maybe Danny was just out of it… maybe he didn't see David at all?*

Mike moved through the lobby and back out onto the street, leaving the Bronxdale Apartments behind him, something he thought he had done years ago. He glanced at his watch. His interview was ten minutes away. There was no way to make it now. He decided to head back home and at least try to salvage any chance he had of getting another appointment. *Maybe if I call down there and make up some story about…SHIT…DAMN IT, David. Fucking damn it!*

He covered the long city blocks quickly. By the time he hit the front door of the house, it was already five minutes past his interview time. He burst into the hallway and stopped in his tracks. It was the smell. He hadn't smelled it since his father had died six years before. Cigarette smoke.

David.

Mike moved into the small kitchen and there he was, seated casually at the table - a cigarette burned to the filter dangling from his fingers, a long, spindly ash waiting to drop from where the rest of the cigarette had been minutes before.

Mike didn't say a word, he just removed his jacket and sat across from his brother.

David was there; his eyes clear but lost in some distant thought. After a second, he looked at Mike and smiled the double-edged smile that hinted at mischief and sincerity at the same time.

"Hey, Mikey," came a voice stronger and more relaxed than Mike expected. "I thought I might have missed you."

Mike was mute from anger, confusion and relief. Seeing David there at the table brought several truths to form. David was alive – which was a relief; and he was back – which was not.

"What are you doing?" Mike asked, without a trace of the churning emotions waiting to vomit forth from his guts.

"Just grabbing a smoke before I head out," answered David calmly.

"Oh," said Mike, nodding his head in mock understanding. "That's good." He paused, gauging his ire, pacing his frustration.

"Nice 'Welcome Home', there, Mikey. I haven't seen you in a while - how about a little small talk, some 'what's going on?' before we slip back into the old routine."

"What's going on? Let's see...oh, yeah, I saw Danny this morning," he said, letting the first volley loose.

David's eyes dropped down into a forlorn stare as he sucked what was left from the dying cigarette. The little orange ember flared desperately and finally died.

"Yeah, I saw him too, last night," he said. "Poor

bastard. He's pretty much gone, huh?"

Mike's resolve began to crack. Bombs away.

"He's gone, Dave? HE'S gone!" Mike shook his head and pressed hard at it with his hands. "Do you have any idea where I just came from? Look at me, David. Look!"

David lifted his eyes from the floor and looked across at Mike, who had pushed himself back from the table, his arms flung wide now.

"Did you notice that I'm wearing a suit? Yeah, so guess where I just came from? I'll give you a little hint- not from the job interview that took me two months to get!"

David's face was blank now, a thin slit taking the place of the smile. He knew Mike would answer for him.

"Yes, David. I put this suit on this morning thinking that I was heading into the city for that interview, because that's how I survive, you know, by working, but instead I was nearly in a fist fight with some CRAZY PUERTO RICAN UP ON TWENTY SEVEN!"

David was still silent but his eyes had grown stronger. He looked hard at his brother.

"What were you doing over there Mike?" came David's words, in a flat voice, not masking a resentful tone.

"Oh, let's see…oh, LOOKING FOR YOU!" erupted Mike.

"You don't need to look for me, Mikey. I'm not like a lost set of keys. I know where I am."

"I don't need to look for you!" Mike was livid. "You know where you are! I know where you are too, now. The only problem with that is you're supposed to be somewhere else."

David's rolled his head slowly on his neck and let it stop in a dead hang in front of him. His hands came up to push it back into place and he looked across at Mike.

"What did you think you were going to find up on that roof, Mikey?"

"I don't know. That's the whole point. I never know what to expect with you."

"Why are you expecting anything with me? Live your own life and leave the expectations for mine alone. Mom's dead a long time, Mikey, and the old man's gone six years now. They didn't leave me to you in the will," said David.

"Yeah, but somehow I inherited you anyway. All your bullshit gets to be my bullshit. All the desperate phone calls come to me. All the cops come to me. Everybody just passes you right back to me like a hot potato."

"You see, that's where the problem is. Nobody can just leave me alone. Everybody has something to say about how I live my life, but they have no follow-through. They bust my balls and then give me some shithouse shuffle," said David simply, without contempt or resentment.

Mike's abating rage flared up again. "Look at me David. Does this look like the SHUFFLE! I'm sitting here, probably flat out of a job I worked really hard to get a shot at because I had to go back up on that damn roof. You know what I expected to find, David. I expected to find you. Just like I always had. You getting all fucked up on whatever you could get your hands on, hanging out, sleeping, hiding, whatever the fuck you do up there. It's you who doesn't follow through. You need a dose of the real world, David."

Mike was unprepared for David's reaction. In his angered state, he wanted fire to greet his own flaming fury, but his brother didn't accommodate. Instead of words of anger, David simply laughed a tired laugh, almost to himself, then spoke softly to his younger sibling.

"The real world, huh, Michael? Maybe that's what's been wrong all along; I don't live in the 'real world'?"

He laughed again and rose from the chair. He moved to the sink and pounded the dead butt into it. He returned to the table, and, still standing, placed his hands flatly down and leaned forward toward where Mike was sitting across from him.

"Where is this real world? Do you live in it, Mikey? Is this where the harsh facts of life come up and slap some sense into you? A 'No Rose-Colored Glasses' zone? Is it some place where people face responsibility and 'fix' their fucked up lives? Nah. The 'real world' is just a threat made to little kids by resentful grown-ups whose own lives suck. A sorry figment of their own miserable imaginations to scare the shit out of each other, a scapegoat for people who want to blame everything on something beyond their own control. "

"Boy, if ever a shoe fit, huh, David!" said Mike.

"Bullshit," David shot back, finally beginning to join with Mike's lonely anger. "I never blamed anything in my life on anybody!"

"So you're telling me that you're fine with the way things are working out?"

"What I'm telling you is that it's my life," David answered plainly. "Some people might not like my choices, but I get to make them. There is no real world, just different people's overlapping little circles, and I get to run my own."

"That would be great if your choices didn't involve anyone else, but they do," Mike shot back. "Just like you said - 'overlapping circles'. Only you don't just overlap, you eclipse people's lives. First Mom and Dad's, and now mine. You know what, David, if I inherited anything it's the old man's ghost."

"You're not gonna' sing that song now, are you? Leave him out of it, Mikey. Just leave him out of it," David said. "I was exactly what he expected. There were no surprises, no disappointments. That's the thing you never got – he knew where I was coming from. He understood. He was more like me than you know."

"I know a lot, David. Living behind you is some long lesson. There was never a subtle wake; there was a debris trail like a tornado had just blown through The Bronx. Believe me I know, David. It got to the point where I could tell that you had been around just by seeing people walking toward me. Not just knowing little hints in people's eyes, there were billboards painted all over their faces –'Guess what your brother did last night!' It's a drag to have to endure someone's pity when I'm angry enough to bash their face in just so I don't have to listen to it. I don't like being 'Poor Mikey'.

"What do you care about what people say? That's their shit, not yours."

"Yeah, but it gets flung on me, David."

"People love to inflict their own misery onto others. They like to twist things up to make themselves feel like somebody else's life is shittier than their own," David said. "I was the perfect foil for their bullshit. I didn't care then and I care even less now. I've only got myself to answer to."

"There you go again," burst Mike. "It's only about you. Did you ever consider that you just might have inflicted yourself on me?"

David's hands brushed away the notion with dismissive waves.

"Life has got to be lived, Michael."

"Is that what you're doing…living? Hiding out on the roof at Twenty Seven?"

"You didn't find me there, did you?" asked David, flatly.

David was right. Mike didn't find him there. This simple fact gave him pause. A hopeful pause in which the runaway train of his morning slowed for a moment.

"I shouldn't be finding you anywhere," he said after a moment of silence.

"You shouldn't be looking, Mikey. We're not kids anymore. You're out looking and worrying about a grown man."

Mike just let his head drop a little lower at this. His shoulders gave just enough for David to notice that something had just hit Mike in a sore spot. He started speaking at the floor but pulled his eyes up to find David's.

"And there it is, David. You missing the whole point, just like always," said Mike, in resurrected defeat.

"What point, Michael. What point did I miss?" David

was no longer argumentative or sarcastic. His question was sincere.

"I'm not looking for a grown man. Even when we were kids, I wasn't looking for some other kid. All along I've just been looking for my brother." Mike's statement seemed to use up all the words that were left.

David lit a fresh cigarette, pulled a long hard draw and let the smoke laze out around his head like a mask. He stared into the white cloud as if he was watching something unfold around him. After the cloud dissipated, he let out another sad laugh.

"Boy, you're really fucked aren't you? I'm all you've got left… I'm sorry about that, Mikey. You don't deserve such a bum deal."

Mike didn't respond to this. He would only be lying to himself if he thought he hadn't felt some truth in David's words.

"What are you doing here, David?"

"I told, you. I was just having a smoke before I head out," David said calmly.

"Head out to where now? I don't think I can go looking for you anymore," said Mike.

David stretched his long arms out, flung his head back hard and yawned so wide it looked as if his skeleton was trying to climb out of his mouth. He walked around and sat next to Mike at the table.

"Stop looking for me, Michael. I appreciate it, and I love you for it, but I have no crumbs to leave behind for you to follow anymore." He put his arm around his brother's shoulder. "I know you're doing what you feel is right, but that's what's right for you, not me. My life is not your burden to bear. Let me pay the price for my own actions. I don't ask for anything from anybody but to be left alone. If I end up locked away somewhere, then that's what's right for me. My soul may be a little brown around the edges, but it's still mine. You know what I'm saying, Mikey?"

As much as Mike wanted to pull away, there was still something reassuring in having David so close. It was either the simple fact that, right now, he did know where his brother was and the gnawing element of uncertainty was gone, or that so much of his own identity was invested in the constant chaos surrounding David that he needed him more than he wanted to admit. The defining element of the whole dynamic between the two was that David didn't grasp the selfishness of his selflessness.

"Doesn't it amaze you how different so many of the people around here turn out?" offered David, slinking back into a profound sag.

"Like us?" asked Mike.

"Not just us, Mikey. Everybody who grows up around here. Maybe it's this neighborhood?" David reached into his head and pulled out a lost memory and laughed a real laugh this time. "Way back - I was probably twelve or something - a bunch of us were climbing the fire-escapes over on the Mildred Apartments and Tommy Mooney slipped and fell like two stories before getting caught up on one of the lower floors. He was hanging like a rag doll - his leg all twisted and bent around the railing, his arms flailing around. He was crazy screaming. It was a sick sound, man. I can still hear it. The rest of us were scared shitless and laughing hysterically at the same time, and then this old man sticks his head out the window right next to us like on the old Batman show when Batman and Robin were fake-climbing the side of a building and Sammy Davis Jr. or some other dick-wad would pop out the window and make some stupid comment..." David laughed harder at this thought, "...anyway, this old man sticks his head out and says, 'You kids are all just a bunch of vicious little monkeys'. Hah! It was too perfect to even be an insult because the old bastard was right. That's what this neighborhood is - a fucking monkey garden filled with vicious little monkeys, every one of us. "

David laughed a little more from inside his memories.

After a few silent moments, he looked long at his brother, leaned in close and put his arm across Mike's shoulder.

"Well, maybe not everyone, Mikey," he said. There was no sarcasm in his statement. It actually contained more hope than Mike realized at the moment.

§

The noon sun seemed to ignore him now as he walked again toward the East 180th Street Station, or maybe he just moved in his own personal sheltering sky since leaving David behind at the house. Mike decided he would be the one to "head out" first. He would be the one walking away this time - the only difference was that he knew no one would ever come looking for him. Something had happened back there at the kitchen table, seeing David, listening to his philosophy on living life free from the expectations of others, unencumbered by the notion that others may be out there somewhere actually giving a shit about what happens to you. He claimed he needed nothing and no one to complete his life. Vagabond - not only in lifestyle, but in soul. Yet oddly enough, he always came back. A disingenuous Diogenes.

How did Danny put it? "He belongs here. This is his home." It was apparently a home that David needed, even more than Mike.

Something had indeed happened this morning, but it hadn't happened to David. It happened to Mike. He let his brother go. Somehow he knew that he would never go looking for David again. He accepted his separation from all the things that tied him to David: the pain, the worry, the grief and the guilt. He accepted all these, yet he didn't feel free. He felt alone. It added a subtle pity to his step, yet he walked on nonetheless.

Mike took in more of surroundings this time as he moved through the neighborhood. He wanted to avoid any more impromptu reunions or casual bullshit sessions. He noticed some people on the street ahead of him and he dropped back an almost indiscernible step. They were clotted outside the Emerald Bar. Though most of his friends should be at work by now, there was still the chance that he knew one of this crowd. He considered crossing the street, but chose not to. He would yield no more ground to any attempt to deter him again today.

As he neared, he realized that he did know the three men outside the bar. One was Jimmy B., the barkeep; one was Jackie Harrington, a New York City firemen and the older brother of Matty Harrington, one of Mike's neighborhood contemporaries; and the other was Joe Morales. Joe was wearing the flat green uniform and orange vest of the New York City Sanitation Department. Mike had worked with Joe some years back as laborers on a big job in the city. He had forgotten that Joe left to become a Sanitation worker. It somehow suited him.

Jimmy noticed Mike as he approached and turned in his direction as he came. Mike knew that he would have to speak first or end up caught again.

"Hey, Jimmy. Resorting to dragging in 'em in off the streets as they pass?" Mike said, with enough of a head start that he could get a laugh and a nod and keep walking.

"Are you kidding? They line up an hour before lunch time for Jimmy B.'s famous corned beef," Jimmy answered. "I might be able to squeeze you in, Mike. But you better hurry before Joey heads in for seconds."

"Nah, Jimmy. Raincheck. I got some where to be," Mike said, his feet still moving.

"Alright. Come back when you shed that suit, Mike," Jimmy ended with his typical big smile.

"You got it, Jimmy."

Mike acknowledged the other men with the generally acceptable street salutation of a nod and a "hey". They reciprocated and turned their attention back to each other. Mike returned his to the sidewalk before him.

He could hear the rumble of the elevated train as he

made his way once again down Adams Street. The short street was empty of people. No barkeeps, firemen, or garbage men.

No Danny.

He was glad.

The abrupt encounter with him earlier had not only changed the course of his day, but possibly his life. He knew that Danny had nothing to do with David's appearance, but he nevertheless wished he had just walked past him, preferring never to have known that David had returned. If only he had kept on walking he could have gone on being "high and mighty" for just a little while longer.

If only…but the vicious little monkeys would surely have none of that.

.

COLLEGE BOY

The outside of Jimmy B.'s was as anonymous as any other neighborhood bar. A brightly lettered, "Emerald Bar", logo was painted on the inside of the long window that shared the brick facade with a heavy wooden door. A tired neon beer sign flickered in endless death throes behind the dark glass. Perched like a keystone above the door, an old, groaning air conditioner baptized the patrons, graciously dripping water onto the heads of those coming and going. The bar blended comfortably with the simple houses that lined both sides of the quiet street.

The inside of the dimly lit barroom was as unremarkable as the outside. The heavy door rushed in behind an entrant like the bellows of a respirator, pumping a life-saving gust of outside air into the still atmosphere of the smoky room. A long, smooth bar ran along the left, its top proudly rubbed dull by the passing of many pilsners.

Behind the bar, the shelves that held the assorted liquor bottles framed an old, murky-edged mirror at whose center was a shoulder height glass shelf that proudly displayed the Black Label society: Jack (Daniels), Johnny (Walker), and Jim (Beam), along with the Maker's Mark, Bushmills and Glenlivet. The Macallan 25 Year was under the counter for special customers only. Below the whiskey was the old metal cash register, and below that, on a low shelf hidden by the shadow of the bar top, was the peace keeper - a Louisville Slugger with the words, "KISS YOUR ASS GOODBYE", etched into the handle.

As faceless as the bar appeared, it was as unique - as was every other neighborhood bar; and what gave it its distinction was its patrons. At the time Jimmy Burke took over the Emerald, the old Bronx neighborhood was waking up again. The nearby city park that had gone quiet after the drugged out days of the Sixties passed was once again a meeting place for the local youth. The Seventies saw Jimmy and his friends come of age on streets stirring with new vitality. There was a spectrum of kids from teens to toddlers laying claim to the neighborhood streets. It was inevitable that the Emerald would be swept up in the change. In a place that had previously catered to a tired generation of lower-class casuals and regular rummies, Jimmy had secured a spot for his fellow former rugrats. Even as the odd leftover lost souls still straggled in, Jimmy's own contemporaries became his first regulars: young working men who needed a place of their own to assemble and unwind. It didn't take long before the Eighties brought their younger brothers and sisters to graduate from their street corners, stoops, and park benches to bar stools in Jimmy B.'s.

Jimmy Burke became the emcee of a lot of the subtle, yet cherished moments in the parade of lives that passed before him. He was the confidante, older brother, guardian angel and tacit spokesman for the new generation of neighborhood youth. His steady voice and large, heavy hands could console or scold - in either case, they were never ignored.

The old Irishman that Jimmy bought the place from knew, and now Jimmy knew - one passing moment in the life of a young man could be a lifeline for the same man in a later time of his own doubt. A time when a man might lose himself in the now, only to find himself again in his past. The Emerald Bar was a depository for the neighborhood's collective soul and Jimmy Burke was the trustee. It was a torch that the old Mick had passed to him without him even knowing, yet one which he proudly bore.

The three young men entered the bar and quickly sat on a group of empty stools by the window. The summer sun was baking the bright world outside and a gust of warm air was pushed through the room as the door rushed to a close behind them. They were all young men barely in their twenties and they were wearing the brightly-colored loose clothing of youth. They joked loudly amongst themselves as they sat awaiting the attention of the barkeep, who was busying himself behind the bar. Their wiry impatience urged them to call out to him, but their haste was tamed by respect. They knew, as did all other patrons of the Emerald Bar, that Jimmy Burke didn't like being shouted at from across the bar. They would wait their turn

Jimmy moved to the far end of the bar and placed a glass neatly on a coaster in front of no one. He poured three fingers of Bushmills for the ghost of Michael Molloy and replaced the whiskey bottle on the shelf behind him.

Before long, Jimmy came over with three draughts and a bowl of pretzels, and placed them in front of the eager young men. Jimmy knew them and didn't need be told what they wanted. They were neighborhood regulars, as were most of the youth of the close knit neighborhood surrounding the bar. Jimmy made it his point to be on a personal level with all the young people in the neighborhood. He was twice the age of the young men in front of him, but he understood them. More years ago than he would ever admit, he was one of them.

"Don't you guys have jobs or something?" Jimmy said with a teasing smile as he stood before the trio.

"Jobs! Jimmy, it's the weekend, my man. I give my forty all week to the man. I gotta' have time to be me," answered one with a smile. He was Johnny Tivoli - "Tiv" to all that knew him - a wisecracking, but good-natured kid that Jimmy liked.

"Be you, huh? Somehow I don't think that's a problem, Tiv. So what *are* you clowns up to today?" Jimmy asked.

"Just a little coolin' off and then out to Jones," replied Tiv

"Jones Beach? Isn't it a little hot out there for the beach?"

"Jimmy, my good man, you just don't get it. You may like sitting in here on a beautiful day, but I've got a duty to share all of this with some of those lonely ladies," he laughed, as he stood up in the bar stool and opened his arms wide.

"I suppose they're just waiting for you out there?" Jimmy laughed.

"You know it. So much skin, so little baby oil. Line 'em up and grease 'em up."

The other two joined in the laughter.

"Things look quiet in here today. We've got room for one more, Jimbo."

"Nah. The beach is not for me. Irish, you know. I sizzle up like bacon. And all that sand in your ass crack. Thanks for the offer boys, but I've got duties of my own."

"Your loss, my good man. But hanging in bars on days like this is for rummies like your buddy over there." Tiv motioned toward the opposite end of the bar. "You don't want me to end up like him, do you?"

Up until then, the other two hadn't noticed the man sitting in the shadows at the far end of the bar. Jimmy didn't need to look. He knew who Tiv was referring to.

"Come on, John. Leave the guy alone," Jimmy's voice was no longer playful. He didn't like shows of disrespect between the different generations that made up his patrons. He looked at the group before him, the latest generation to come up from the playgrounds and onto his stools. They weren't so different from the last group, or Jimmy's own group before that. The characters of the never-ending tale of The Bronx always seemed to stay the same. Dean Santo, the guy at the end of the bar, was no exception.

"Okay, Okay. I'm only messing around, Jimmy." Tiv swallowed down the last of the beer and placed the empty glass on the bar. "Come on, Gents. It's time for some fun in the sun. They'll be lined up five deep by three o'clock. Hey, maybe I can get one of their mother's phone numbers for you, Jimmy," he laughed as he headed for the door.

The other two followed suit and laughed among themselves as they exited back out into the bright world beyond the window of the bar.

Jimmy stared out into the beating sun for a second longer after Tiv and the others left and then turned back to the bar. He filled a beer glass and walked slowly down to the far end. He placed the cool glass on a small round coaster in front of the lone man who was lost somewhere in his thoughts as Jimmy approached. Jimmy knew what brought Dean to the dark end of his bar. The story had made the rounds of the neighborhood years back when it happened, just one more chapter in the living novel that was The Bronx.

No, Tiv, he thought. *I don't want you to end up like him.*

§

Silence and smoke filled the old Plymouth Fury, its four occupants sunk as deeply into the darkness as they were into the tired seats. The car was parked tightly against the curb beside a small city park. The park itself was no more than a fenced in asphalt playground ringed with a single row of unremarkable trees, a complement of exhausted painted wooden benches, and a hard-worn sidewalk, yet it embodied more than any casual observation could discern. It was a legacy for kids growing up in each neighborhood of the city to have a local place to call their own. A shared, yet personal place - not only in space, but in time as well. A place to provide and safeguard the necessary memories of youth before social circles came of age and innocence diminished to responsibility. The park was a place of ownership and identity for those growing up in the neighborhood. Each park and each neighborhood as distinct as they were similar. A starting place and jump-off point from childhood to teen years, though teens and beyond still gathered long after they had outgrown its swings and slides.

The neighborhood park was a Neo-Neverland for urban Lost Boys.

The day had receded and the children of the light were long asleep, their cheery voices deferred until the next day's sport, as the backdrop of their shining existences yielded to an undisturbed arena of night shadows unleashed by the dim street lamps overhead. The swings were still; the seesaws were balanced in awkward states of equilibrium; the monkey bars were an empty steel framework; and the slide, always the proud symbol of the playground, stood tall and fearless against the night. The only intrusions on the calm that blanketed the street were the signs of near-life inside the car as a lone voice finally nudged the stillness.

"Well, I'm not going to sit here all night. What do you say I just drop you guys off…even if you could probably *walk* home faster?"

The question hung motionless inside the old car, buoyed on the thinning veil of marijuana smoke, unable to land on comprehending ears.

With no response promising, Tommy, the car's driver, straightened himself from his protracted slouch and cranked the ignition.

Suddenly, as if struck by some unseen blow, the Lost Boys became aware. Almost in unison the two in the backseat bemoaned the apparent ending of the night.

"Hey, man," moaned Riff. "It's too early to go home."

"Too early," seconded Danny, with a matter-of-fact tone and an accompanying farcical nod.

"Too early if you've got nothing to do and nowhere to

go. I'm kinda' burnt and I've got a full schedule of classes tomorrow."

"Sorry, College Boy," came a sharp voice from beside him in the passenger seat. Dean spat the words as he continued gazing out his window. He hadn't partaken of the pipe passing on this night, but he was as distant as the heavy-toking Danny. He had spent most of the night lost somewhere just beyond the glass of the window.

Tommy looked over at Dean with a deepening scowl. His friend had struck a chord that he had clearly struck many a time before. A rekindled frustration had surfaced in Tommy's eyes.

"You know, Dean, it's always the same shit with you. It's getting old."

"Sorry, if *we've* got nowhere to go," Dean said, without looking over at Tom. "We're just a few guys with *nothing* to do tomorrow."

"Don't twist my words or my balls because I'm doing something besides sitting around all day feeling sorry for myself then getting high all night," Tommy shot back. "It's called 'life'. You should try it, Dean. You could ease into it. You might even start with a job."

Danny and Riff began cackling like demented children in the back seat. "Ooh," they called and laughed.

"Start with a job, bitch," mimicked Riff.

"Yeah, a job," echoed Danny.

Dean let his gaze fall from the window into his lap. His face held a small, unfriendly smile. He looked over at Tom, who met his eyes unwaveringly.

"Tom-Tom, the College Boy. Gonna' be somebody and move outta' this lousy neighborhood," he said, with a sarcastically emphasized Bronx accent. "Gonna' leave us losers behind."

"Fuck you, Dean," responded Tommy instantly. "Loser is your word, man, not mine."

The comic mocks from Danny and Riff hit a high shriek at Tom's parley. They whispered an exaggerated, "*looooser*," from behind Dean's seat and hushed a joint fit of hysterical laughter. They were a demented Rosencrantz and Guildenstern.

"Right," Dean responded coolly, ignoring the idiots in the backseat, and returned his gaze to the window. "Let's just call it a night. We wouldn't want to make you miss the school bell, Tom."

"Ding, dong," came another backseat chortle followed by more hushed laughs.

Tom's face crunched and his head swung away as he talked. "I must be nuts. I must be fuckin' nuts," he said aloud to himself. "I go to school all week, I work just as much. I have hardly any time to myself, and this is how I spend it!"

As Dean sat staring out one window, and Tommy talked to himself; Danny and Riff conspired in their backseat neutrality. Danny produced a near empty plastic baggie of marijuana.

"Not enough for a bowl, but plenty for a bone!" he happily proclaimed.

He excitedly emptied it into a waiting rolling paper in Riff's fingers. Soon the distinct smell of burning marijuana once again wafted around the tense air of the car. Tommy smelled it long before it brought him back from the edge of his anger.

"What the hell are you guys doing?" he asked, annoyed that his friends were not taking him seriously.

"They're losers, Tom. What did you expect?" Dean spoke from his faraway place in the window. Tommy shrugged his shoulders and shook his head at Dean's taunting. He didn't want to get into a fight with Dean, but he didn't like being pushed. He glanced back at Danny and Riff, expecting to convey his ire, but was disarmed by the immanent, innocent humor of the comic duo.

"We need to lighten the mood in here, man," answered Danny, with a sincere face.

"Yeah, lighten up," doubled Riff, now swapping roles

as an echo with Danny.

Danny passed the glowing white stick over the seat back, but Tommy waved it off. Dean didn't even acknowledge Danny's hand. Danny shrugged and brought it to his own lips. He drew deeply, brightening the orange ember to the intensity of a small sun. He passed the greatly reduced bone over to Riff, all the while holding his breath tightly in his chest. He spoke as he let the smoke slowly exit his lungs.

"Come on, Tom! Let's go for a cruise," offered Riff.

"Yeah, cruise," came the muffled support of Danny, still reveling in the throes of his glassy-eyed euphoria.

"No. No cruising." Tommy's brow crunched slightly as he derided his backseat patrons, but he instantly felt bad about snapping at them. He wasn't keen on one of their mindless excursions, but he began to feel bad about what had transpired between him and Dean and thought a ride might cool things off. Although Dean had pounded at him, Tommy knew that Dean was really more upset with himself than with him or the others.

Where there was truth in what Tommy said to Dean, there may have also been some in what Dean said to Tommy. Tommy didn't view his friends as losers, and these three were his oldest friends, but he was disappointed in their lack of ambition. As young boys growing up, they had learned about life together. From the schoolyard as kids, to the streets as teens, and out the windows of cars as young men; they explored the city as one and awakened the conceit of youth that would be needed to temper the ignorance of adulthood.

Through all that they suffered at each other's hands, the four were close; changed, but still close.

Tommy started the car and pulled away from the curb.

"One quick ride and that's it," he said, in reluctant surrender.

"Yeah!" called Danny and Riff together, like two small children on a Sunday drive, and they began to bounce and sing, "We're off to see the Wizard". They were harmless to all but themselves; unwittingly assuming their inevitable role in Spencer's great dance of societal survival.

Dean stared at his faraway place in the window as if he wasn't even in the car.

The air inside the car was silent again as it moved along with the night under the elevated Bruckner Expressway. Overhead a rib cage of steel beams criss-crossed the exposed underside of the heavy roadway that was held up by steel and concrete pillar-legs, each standing tall and disappearing up into shadows. The roadway above gave a rolling growl with each unseen vehicle passing on its rough skin, haunting the air in the makeshift canyon below with fleeting echoes.

A long, dividing median split the wide street under the expressway. This urban atoll was strewn with lost mufflers, the odd discarded tire, and scattered, unremarkable trash. It was pockmarked from where the old cobblestones that made up its surface had been looted. Some of these large, heavy stones had likely found their way into the suburban homes of apostate Bronx-ites as garden pathways or fireplaces - keepsakes from a place left behind, but quietly longed for. Tommy even had one in his bedroom as a doorstop; the rough-edged gray stone keeping him from being shut in, or shut out.

Tommy took in his slowly passing surroundings: the rusting green-gray steel work above him, the few remaining cobblestones along the roadway divider, the pale yellow light cast by the street lamps, the mix of dingy apartment buildings and industrial warehouses lining the roadway on either side, just close enough to be swallowed by the shadow of the overhead expressway. They all lent to the collective loneliness pervading the nighttime backdrop.

A few blocks deeper into Hunt's Point would expose a sadly common element of city life - surrendered streets. Streetwalkers, junkies, drug dealers - all parading the streets, defying passersby not to look, or even touch. They were like cockroaches with no fear of the lights. They would not scatter, they would gather in even greater numbers.

They had become a grim fact of life in Hunt's Point.

During the day, cars and trucks would rumble and roar along Hunt's Point Avenue, making their way to destinations throughout the busy Bronx neighborhood. The Terminal Market - the city's hub of fruit and vegetable distribution - kept the streets filled with produce trucks coming and going, adding to the steady flow of gasoline and oil trucks streaming along the busy service roads. Auto salvage and scrap metal yards scattered among the side streets provided a thriving marketplace for the steady stream of curbside mechanics and junkmen. Auto glass and body shops set up their homes in old warehouses that were left over from the days when the railroads were the dominant industry in this old part of New York City's northern most borough. Businesses and buildings always found a way to recycle themselves in Hunt's Point. It was a collective industrial park long before the idea became the adopted child of uninspired city planners. Days were long and fully consumed by the round-the-clock engine of trade. Sunset signified nothing more than the awakening of street lamps, and the changing of the guard.

As dark descended, the industrial zone around the Terminal Market became a bazaar of all things unsavory, yet unavoidable, in any hardscrabble city neighborhood. Urban decay and its co-dependent economy of "don't ask, don't tell" were equally industrious in Hunt's Point. The currency of the night was misery and submission. Whores, transvestites, and drug peddlers flashed their goods and talked trash to every passing vehicle. There was a free sideshow under every dim street lamp. It wasn't unusual to find cars filled with curious young boys from the "better" parts of The Bronx sightseeing alongside men harboring darker pursuits. Riding around Hunt's Point was a cheap and accessible urban amusement park; and a glut of life's sordid lessons as well. Flesh and soul were up for grabs on any given night.

Tommy had made this trip many times since he and the others had gained access to their parent's cars - with or without their consent. It was almost a rite of passage for young boys to take a trip into Hunt's Point at night and get a glimpse of a street-corner, sex-hawker or a flamboyant transvestite. It was fodder for park bench chatter and schoolyard exotica.

While at first intriguing, for Tommy, the trips quickly became mundane, and finally somewhat heartbreaking. He quietly held a nostalgic romanticism for the simpler, purer days of the city.

The arrival of the subway in the early part of the century heralded rapid development in this part of the Bronx. The small farms that once quilted the landscape had disappeared under wide apartment buildings and open fields were filled with industry. Most of the older buildings were demolished.

The ravenous development of a city has an appetite for its own past

Even the once great homes of Hunt's Point were victims of the slow march of time. There was the grand Casanova mansion - a huge house once nicknamed 'Whitlock's folly' after its original owner, who was ridiculed by his neighbors for building such a conspicuous manse. Casanova was a successful Cuban sugar and coffee planter who purchased the home from the Whitlock estate, and then quietly proceeded to use it as a storage depot for rifles and gunpowder. It was eventually abandoned and demolished to make way for a piano factory.

Tommy often came down to Hunt's Point alone, no longer out of youthful curiosity for the sordid goings on, but to think among the old buildings and streets. They called out to him, and calmed him. They cleared his mind and refreshed his spirit. He would scan the darkened buildings and the faint skyline above him for the subtlest traces of past grandeur. He loved the old brick structures for their persistence and refusal to crumble under the weight of change. He was thrilled by things like old cement cornices and ornate iron railings, even though they were mostly covered with grime or years of flaking paint and rust. He knew where all the old estates once were, and where the farms once were.

Again, he felt at home in the places that most others chose to flee; places that were abandoned not out of hopelessness, but out of fear of being left behind. Tommy was an admirer in a museum no one else seemed to see.

Danny and Riff had fallen into a euphoric crash-sleep in the backseat, heads on each other's shoulders like two young children on a long car ride. Dean was blinking slowly into the reflections of the night on the glass of the window.

Tommy looked in the rear-view mirror and saw his sleeping children-friends, and looked over at Dean. He was no longer upset with Dean. He wanted to break the ice that had built up earlier.

"Hey, Dean. Ever wonder about the old days of the city?"

Dean spoke from the glass. "Same shit, Tom. Just a long time ago."

"Nah," he said lightly, steering clear of an argument. "This place was great. There were shops all along here, and a trolley running right along the way we're driving. Horse-drawn carts, man. Even a two-room schoolhouse. Check that out."

Dean didn't seem interested. He had heard Tommy's ramblings on the subject before. Tommy's face began to flush with childlike excitement as he spoke.

"How about this - this part of The Bronx was once the hub of piano building for the whole country. There were piano factories all over the place."

Dean broke his silence, but didn't share Tommy's

enthusiasm, or his nostalgic streak.

"Spare me the history lesson, Tom. Look at it now." Dean's hands gestured with dismissal at the world outside his window. "Here's The Bronx in all its glory, my friend: busted up buildings, burned out car shells, pimps and whores, garbage all over the place…and stupid idiots like us cruisin' around in it, pretending like it's not real, like it's here to amuse us when we're bored. The only shops around here now are the trunks of cars and back alleys, and it ain't pianos that they're selling. You want to shop, go to 5ᵗʰ Avenue. You want dope or some skanky ass - you're in the right place."

Tom frowned at Dean's dark assessment. He saw what Dean saw, but he also saw what was underneath. He saw the heart of the streets. He saw the spirit. He felt it as well. He was connected with the city right down into his bones. Even in the downtrodden neighborhoods, he felt something calling him, drawing him in. Where most people would be afraid to even pass through some parts of The Bronx in a car, Tommy felt safe walking around. He knew that the people who walked in the shadows of these busy roads, who lived in the decaying buildings, felt it too. He didn't fear the streets.

Tommy didn't deny the viciousness of the city, or the dark side of the streets, but he wouldn't let that blind him to the subtle purity that survived under the harsh exterior.

"You know why The Bronx ain't burning anymore, Tom? Because it's not worth it. Even the scumbags don't give a shit anymore," Dean posed.

"What happened to you, Dean? When did you become so gloomy?" Tommy asked with sincere concern.

"I'm not gloomy. I'm realistic," Dean responded without his usual sarcasm.

He turned from the window and looked at Tommy. He knew his friend was always looking for the good in a situation, but he didn't share Tommy's optimism. Dean saw the world through eyes that had learned cynicism from the streets he grew up on. He saw the innocent neighborhood rivalries that usually ended in schoolyard scuffles fester into senseless brutal border wars that would never end, cycles of violence that just grew bigger with each passing summer. He watched as young people - some friends, some not - died for no reason other than they were in the wrong place at the wrong time, their blood spilling onto the streets that should have been their hope, not their fate. He saw innocent youthful curiosity and experimentation slide into rabid drug addiction. He watched as the expectancy of hope for a simple life of good work and good money crumble under the weight of unemployment and heavy competition for unskilled positions. The days of easing into a good civil service job - an opportunity always taken for granted - were lost in the haze of equal employment and quotas. He watched as rising real estate prices even took away any prospect for his future residence in his own neighborhood. His only chance for a future was to deny the future itself. He wouldn't change with the times; he would stay nowhere for as long as he could. He would hold back the march of time by turning his back on it, but the price he would pay would be the choice itself. He denied the future, so he would never have one.

"I'm like a mirror, you know? I'm just a reflection of what's going on around me," Dean continued softly. He looked again for his reflection in the glass of the car window but only saw the darkness of the night outside.

"That's a load of crap, Dean," Tom responded, losing the calm he had hoped to retain. He didn't want to preach to Dean but he couldn't let his friend surrender so willingly. "We've grown up in the same place, and you don't here that kind of shit from me."

"You're a dreamer, Tom. You think everything is fine, everything is gonna' be okay. If that's what makes things real for you, then that's great. You keep thinking that."

"It's all in how you look at things," Tom said.

"I can't look anymore. I guess I've got lazy eye."

"More of the same old bullshit, Dean," Tommy said flatly.

Dean found himself in a role reversal with Tom. Dean was now the calm one trying not to hurt his friend, and Tom was smoldering. He spoke with tones of resolution.

"I don't mean to insult you, Tommy. I think it's great that you can feel that way, but it'll never happen for me. I got sucked in a long time ago, man. I just don't have what it takes, you understand?" Dean looked Tommy in the eyes as he spoke his last line and made a silent plea for acceptance.

"No, I don't understand. I have no fucking clue what you're talking about," Tommy said. "You're talking like an old man looking back on some hard knock life." He wanted to be angry with Dean, but his fire was extinguishing before it could even spark.

"No, not looking back, just looking ahead," Dean answered.

He looked at Dean and suddenly saw the young boy that he had first met in a schoolyard fade into a shade before his eyes. He did understand, but didn't want to believe. With a sad nod and a long sigh, he released his friend from the added weight of his hopes for him. Tommy slowly turned his gaze back toward the windshield and the black road slowly passing under the wheels of the car.

Dean turned from Tommy and again stared out the window. His reflection in the glass joined him anew.

Tommy turned mindlessly from the wide, brightly-lit Hunt's Point Avenue onto one of the narrower side streets that cut down toward the more industrial zone of the Point, trading the echoes and shadows of the elevated expressway for the gray silence of the night.

He could have continued straight on and meet a larger street, but Tommy liked his little diversions through the lesser streets of Hunt's Point. It got to the point where he just randomly turned onto streets hoping to come upon something he had never seen before, or missed on a previous trip. Tommy reached the corner and realized he was at Lafayette Street.

Outside his window was the Valencia Bakery, an old style bakery that made all kinds of sheet cakes and special occasion cakes. Tommy's father once brought him here as a boy to pick up a cake for a big party at his job, and Tommy was thrilled. He felt as if he had been introduced to a magical place that no one else knew about. The tall spires of the wedding cakes and the mountains of icing flowers enchanted him.

Tommy cheered at the sight of the old bakery, but it faded quickly under the growing heaviness he felt as he looked out across the street. A lone functioning street-lamp cast little light on the corner, but it was enough to see that the street was empty. Tommy lightly shook his head, as if to shake out the uneasiness that had crept up into it from his chest The sounds of the city played low in the distance, the din of cars and trucks passing on the elevated Bruckner Expressway now buzzed somewhere behind him like invisible pests, but the streets themselves seemed still. Not silent, just warily quiet. And the quiet seemed to be everywhere.

On this night, Tommy couldn't seem to appreciate his private collection. He looked at the old buildings, but didn't see anything but old buildings. Something had settled on his heart and made him uneasy.

Maybe it's just Dean, he thought. What he said was pretty heavy. He looked over at his friend who was lost again in the world of the windshield glass, and felt saddened. *These guys can't feel that hopeless*, he thought. *We're all so young. Too young to give up.* Tommy vowed silently to spend more time with Dean. He had to get through to him. He would be the one to get out, but he was going to bring them all with him, not leave them behind.

He glanced into the rear-view mirror at his almost forgotten friends in the backseat. Danny and Riff were sound asleep. Danny's head had slipped from Riff's shoulder and now rested peacefully in his lap. A small smile lifted the corners of Tommy's lips. He felt a chuckle rising from the comical sight of his two jester-like friends. *Too young*, he thought again, and his smile flattened.

He suddenly felt very tired. The initial somberness of the trip and the heaviness of Dean's statements began to wear heavy on Tommy. He just felt like going on home and shutting down for the night. He looked over at Dean, whose gaze had shifted from the front windshield to the side window. Dean seemed to be struggling to see through the glass, like a sighted man suddenly gone blind.

"Hey, Dean. What do you say we call it a night? I'm kinda' tired and there doesn't seem to be much of anything going on down here tonight," Tommy said softly, almost pleadingly.

It took a moment for the words to register with Dean. He heard them, but took a moment to understand them. He had been lost in thoughts of his own while Tommy was driving. Pulled back from the world of the window, his thoughts went back into the head of the reflection Dean had seen in the glass.

"What, Tom?" Dean paused, struggling with the words. "Yeah. Yeah, sure. There's nothing going on and I'm tired myself."

Dean remembered the others and turned to look over the backseat. He laughed when he saw the sight of the two sleeping young men. Riff's mouth had fallen open, and a small strip of drool from his hanging lower lip had connected itself to Danny's neck.

"Look at these two," he laughed. "Now there's a picture. You gotta' start keeping a camera in this car, Tom."

Tommy glanced over his shoulder and smiled at the sight. He then looked over at the laughing Dean and smiled wider. He also wished he had a camera at this moment, more for a picture of a laughing Dean than of the other two. They always provided amusing scenarios, but Dean laughed all too infrequently these days.

Tommy let himself hold onto the moment for a while longer, then looked back out across the street. Seeing that they were still the only car, he pressed lightly on the gas pedal and slipped around the corner.

He could see the brighter lights of Halleck Street – the road that lead back out of Hunt's Point and up to the Bruckner Expressway service road - at the far end of the street. Danny and Riff were still asleep in the back seat, and Dean was sitting with his head hung back into the headrest, his eyes closed in thought. Tommy was pretty much alone with the streets as he drove along, but he didn't mind; the path was well worn enough for him to drive home blindly.

With a familiar end in sight, Tommy relaxed and began to lose himself in his own thoughts. The events of the night were cleansing; the words were harsh, but the feelings were pure. He was glad that the air was somewhat cleared between him and Dean, even at the cost of some long held hopes between the two. He wondered if he and Dean weren't thinking the same thing.

The scenery of the night passed unnoticed as the car moved along on the shadowy street. Tommy was finished with his sightseeing and was more concerned with getting home. As he drove through the last empty intersection, his eyes casually scanning the last stretch of street between him and the road home, he caught sight of another car up ahead that he hadn't really noticed a moment ago. It drew his attention because it was up on the sidewalk, the front corner of the car slightly crunched into the brick wall of the building that occupied the left side of the street. One of the headlights still shone, but Tommy couldn't make out any signs of people in or around the car. He wondered if it was an accident, but then he began to feel uneasy and for an instant he wondered if he shouldn't just quickly back out and avoid the street entirely.

With the service road so near, he decided to continue on - he was suddenly very eager to get out of Hunt's Point.

He slowed as he approached the scene, his eyes wary of the shadows outside.

Dean opened his eyes as he felt the car slow; his thoughts still half occupying his mind. "What's going on?" he asked as he tried to focus on his surroundings.

"I don't know, but I don't like it. I'm just gonna' get out of here as quick as I can."

Dean spotted the car against the wall and moved forward from his reclining position. He looked into the shadows surrounding the crashed vehicle. He could see that its driver's door was flung wide in haste. The inside of the car was palely illuminated by its weakly burning interior dome light. He could see that the car was empty, but the scene felt fresh. Whoever was in that car had to be nearby.

"Probably some crack head all fired up," said Dean, dismissing the scene.

"Yeah, but where is he?" Tommy scanned the opposing sidewalks.

Tommy's car was almost upon the other car when he was surprised by the sudden emergence of a man from the deep shadows. Tommy couldn't see his face, but he could feel his angry eyes upon him. He thought he could almost see two burning yellowish slits where the man's eyes should be.

As Tommy was looking across him and out the passenger side window, Dean was in turn looking into the darkness outside Tommy's window. They were now right across from the other car, and Dean was gazing into the shadows around it. He didn't feel the urgency that Tommy did, but his curiosity was engaged. He hadn't gotten to see any "freaks" on the trip, so he felt a glimpse of a broken up crack head would be a fair consolation prize. He was quickly disappointed by the absence of any such creature and was about to return his head to its place of rest on the seat when he caught a sudden motion low to the ground. As he strained to see into the darkness, he was wrenched away by Tommy's sudden proclamation of, "Oh, shit!"

"What the hell?" called out Dean, suddenly not so casual in the face of the unexpected changes in the night around him. He also caught sight of the man coming out of the shadows. "Let's get the hell out of here Tom. I don't like the looks of this guy."

"You're tellin' me," answered Tommy in agreement.

Just as he was about to slam down on the gas pedal, the spidery fabric of the street drew them into its web. The back door behind Tommy opened unexpectedly and he hit the brakes in surprised reaction. Dean, whose eyes were fixed on the approaching man, was hurled against the dashboard as the car lurched and then jerked back.

"What the fuck is going on!" Dean shouted, losing his composure in the rapidly accelerating mayhem. He turned toward Tommy who was staring with disbelief over the seat back.

Danny was the first of the two slumbering backseat passengers to respond to the rough wake-up call of the surging and stopping of the car. His body flew forward, pinching Riff's head between his chest and the back of the seats in front of him. The snap of his own head startled him into consciousness. He couldn't recall exactly where he was, his head still light with induced euphoria. He was trying to focus through the dim light inside the car when he felt something grip his leg.

Crawling into the back of the car was a bleeding, half-naked woman. Her sparse clothing was ripped and hanging from her beaten body. She had pulled herself into the car and onto the laps of the groggy duo who were slowly recovering from their sudden rousing.

"You gotta' help me. He's gonna' kill me," she mumbled as best should could through swollen lips.

Riff woke to the dull pain in his head from where it was pressed into the seat back. Holding his head in his hands, he sat back. As he slowly opened his eyes, he turned toward Danny. He was about to spew at his inconsiderate friend when he caught sight of the woman wriggling toward him across Danny's lap. "WHOA!" he cried as he jumped back from this strange apparition. Danny was stiff with a mixture of shock and disbelief.

Dean, succumbing to an urgent panic, remembered the man outside the car.

"WHERE THE HELL IS HE?" he shouted as his head swung, nervously searching the night outside the glass.

Dean spun around in his seat as he desperately sought the man. Tommy was still staring into the back at the woman who had made her way fully into the car.

"WHERE IS HE, TOM?" Dean's voice was almost a shriek.

The scene inside the car was one of frenzy. Dean was shouting, Riff was bouncing up and down in his seat. Danny was frozen with fear, and Tommy was twisting wildly in the fray.

"WHO THE HELL IS SHE?" yelled Tommy at no one.

Dean, frantically scanning the dark street around them, reached over and grabbed Tommy's shoulder. "WHO CARES, JUST GO. GET OUT OF HERE. NOW!"

Tommy smashed the gas pedal into the floor and the car leaped forward, throwing them all back against their seats, and splaying the strange woman flatly in the laps of Danny and Riff. The two lifted their arms high above the woman, afraid to touch her bruised and beaten body.

It was as the car surged that Dean caught sight of the man. He saw him emerge from the shadows of the crashed car and hurry toward the street in front of them. In the faint light, Dean thought he saw the outline of a long gun. His heart pounded in his chest and he instinctively reached for the steering wheel.

Tommy's face was white and his eyes bulged with fear as he now also saw the man plant himself in the path of the car. He felt the car suddenly veer left, the steering wheel being forced from his grip. The shadowy man left his line of vision and the bricks of the wall came up on him quickly. As he tried to regain control of the car, the windshield shattered into tiny cubes, some driving into the skin of his neck and face. Tommy grabbed the steering wheel and yanked it hard to the right. He heard a loud bump as something heavy bounced off of the car. Bright lights hammered down on him suddenly, and he realized he was now on Halleck Street. He turned blindly and buried the gas pedal, propelling the car with a sharp chirp and then a bellowing roar.

With his heart racing along with the car, he peered into the rear view mirror, fearing pursuit. From the receding scene of the mirror, he called over to Dean.

"I don't see him," he said excitedly, but not relieved.

In the mirror, he noticed Danny and Riff both cringing with their arms wrapped around their heads. He swung his head back to the street before him, suddenly realizing that most of the windshield was gone. The cool night aired poured in through a huge, ragged hole and rushed around his face and across his chest. Tommy had never seen a shotgun blast in person, but he was pretty sure that was what had just shattered his windshield. The shadow man must have gotten off a round before they tore past him.

"Dean, what the hell happened back there?" He spoke as he drove, not looking over at his friend. Dean didn't respond. Tommy spared a quick glance over toward Dean, and as his eyes fell upon him he slammed on the brakes.

Dean's head was flung back against the seat. His eyes were wide and blank, staring out the hole in the windshield. Small cuts all over his face were swelling with red drops.

"Dean!" called Tommy, twisting his body toward him as the car came to a stop.

"DEAN!" he called again nervously. He reached out to grab his friend by the shoulders and pull him around, but as his hands gripped him, Tommy could feel something wrong. The hand that he sent out to grasp Dean's shoulder sunk into loose, wet flesh. Tommy's fingers immediately loosened as he felt what he knew to be the bone of Dean's arm. Tommy stretched across the body of his friend and his face twisted with both fear and sickness.

Most of the flesh of Dean's right upper arm was gone. Tommy could see the white of bone through the strands of remaining skin. Blood soaked the entire side of his body. Tommy began to panic, but knew that if his friend was going to live he would have to act quickly. He looked over the back seat at Danny and Riff who seemed lost in some kind of shock.

"Riff," he shouted. "RIFF! Reach over here and hold Dean. Hold him against the seat. Do you hear me? Hold him down."

Riff shook his head, trying to come around. He couldn't believe what had just happened; he was jolted awake and thrust into a nightmare. In a matter of seconds, he had a battered woman crawl onto him, and seemingly out of nowhere, for reasons he would probably never know, some maniac had blasted Tommy's car apart and Hell had rushed in through the broken windshield.

Tommy's urgency somehow reached deep down into Riff and dragged him into consciousness. He mindlessly responded, lowering his arms and reaching forward to grasp Dean by the shoulders. He felt the warm stickiness of Dean's damaged arm, but he resisted the urge to pull away and held him fast. Riff looked down at the woman sprawled across him and Danny, and shook his head in disbelief. Danny was lost beside him with his head buried somewhere under the tangle of his raised arms. He watched as the night raced along outside the car windows in a shadowy blur as Tommy sped away. Tommy's fascination with the old Bronx neighborhood had given him some practical knowledge besides the nostalgic - he knew the area well enough to find Lincoln Hospital.

The night moved in to swallow the void left by the retreating car.

§

"I think we're better off in here today, Dean. It looks pretty hot out there."

The man looked up at Jimmy from his slumped position at the bar. "Yeah," he offered plainly. He sipped the fresh beer quietly and placed it on its coaster, the soft thump magnified by the quickly re-established silence. Jimmy hated being uncomfortable in his own place, but he didn't walk away. He needed something more from the man before he could be released. The bartender's code bound him to be an ear for those that no one else would listen to. He knew that no one had listened to Dean Santo for a long time.

Dean looked down into his glass and finally spoke softly, "I heard from Tommy the other day." Jimmy could see the bittersweet taste that the mention of his old friend brought to Dean's lips. "He's a partner now in that firm. Imagine that, huh. Tommy's a big time architect." Dean masked his quivering voice with a forced laugh.

"No kidding," said Jimmy lightly. "He was always a bright kid. He's up in Westchester somewhere?"

"Yeah," said Dean. "I guess he kinda' outgrew the old neighborhood."

Jimmy began to think better of the way the conversation was leading; he didn't want to hit any nerves about guys who moved on, or guys who got left behind.

"He got married too, didn't he?" Jimmy sidestepped. "That's usually the clincher. Women and money change a man more than anything else in this world." Good move, he thought. *Standard safe bullshit conversation.*

"I wouldn't know about either," said Dean.

Code or not, Jimmy opted to bail out. "Me neither," he added with a lame forced chuckle. He tapped the bar in front of him and said, "You need anything to munch on down here?"

Dean shrugged off the offer.

"Okay, let me go work on these glasses. The damn dishwasher is broken. I have to do them all by hand."

Jimmy headed down to the other end of the long bar, reached into the wide sink beneath it and began washing glasses that were already clean.

Dean was still lost in his thoughts as Jimmy walked away. He mindlessly lifted his left hand, brought it across his chest and grasped his withered limb. Where his left arm was thick and muscled just below the shoulder, his right was thin and weak. He couldn't lift it without help from his left. He could barely raise his hand to his waist, and couldn't do much with it when he got it there. He pinched the shrunken bicep with the strong fingers of his left hand. It felt like a wet dishtowel. *Why did they have to save it?* He often wished they had just cut it off after the shooting. It only hung from his body like a cruel joke. The arm that he couldn't even write his name with had become his signature.

Dean thought about the years that had passed since the night in Hunt's Point. Tommy had gone on with his plans, and so had he. That night wasn't a "fateful" one for Dean; his shooting was no life-altering event. The whole thing was a simple affirmation of what his life was meant to be. The real tragedy would have been if the shot had blasted Tom; then the balance of things would have been fucked. Tommy was bound to do something better, to make something of his life. But the lead and glass found Dean and all was right with the world. He knew this to be true and it was in this thought that he found the only comfort he was due. His shitty life was his contribution to the program. Nothing as noble as self-sacrifice; just his turn to ante up.

All was right with the world.

That long ago night was an education for Dean. He was a "college boy" too, just like Tommy. Ten years of a dreamless existence was his curriculum.

Dean Santo was right where he belonged, with nothing to do and nowhere to go.

He pulled his wasted arm up on to the bar top and wrapped his weak fingers around the beer glass and closed his eyes. He imagined himself raising the glass in a toast.

"Here's to you, Tom," he said so softly he probably only heard the words in his own head..

REMNANTS

Jimmy B. moved through the narrow alley behind the bar. It was his space and his alone. His sanctuary, his pulpit; his dugout, his safe house. Nothing could touch a bartender behind his bar. When you're a waiter, you're in somebody else's house, but when you are bartender, everybody's in your house. The Emerald Bar was Jimmy's house and he surveyed it with his own Eye of Providence before making his way to the far end of the bar where a small group of guys were having an animated conversation.

"Everything good down here?" he asked, lifting glasses and wiping the bar.

"Everything is always good, Jimmy, my man," answered Johnny Tivoli. "We were just discussing the finer points of life and we concluded that our friend Phil here is essentially what you might call, uh...a fucking bum."

Two young men were standing alongside two other men seated in bar-stools. The "bum" in question, was one of the men seated.

One of the standing men, Sean Murphy, needled the antagonist, "You mean *you* concluded, Tiv," as he drew a sip from his glass.

"That's a little harsh, wouldn't you say, John?" said

Jimmy, reaching across the bar, offering a consoling rub of the young man in question's shoulder. "Maybe Phil's just a late bloomer."

"Harsh! Late bloomer! Jimmy, Phillie hasn't had a job since we all worked at the Hess Station over on Boston Post Road when we were seventeen. That was over three years ago. How fucking sorry is it when you're still grubbing beer money from your mother!"

The two other men chuckled loudly as they sipped from half-filled pilsners.

"Please Tiv. Like that's any different from you grubbing beer money from us?" Sean countered.

Johnny responded, "That's not grubbin', that's 'feeding the wheel'. I feed the wheel when *you're* busted, other times you kick in. That's why it's called the *wheel*, and that's why when fellows like Phil here don't feed it, the wheel grinds to a halt. So it's left up to us, or in this case, Phil's *mom*, to pick up his slack."

The long 'oooh's' from the others accented the low-blow. Phil took it all in stride with another slow sip from his beer.

"Easy on the 'mother' stuff, Johnny," came a casual rebuff from Jimmy.

Tiv conceded a nod to Jimmy B. The big man liked to keep things from getting out of hand in his house and Johnny Tivoli was clearly testing the limits.

"You're right. You're right, Jimmy. Phil's mother shouldn't take the hits for her boy. I mean, it's not her fault. There's a very simple scientific explanation for our friend here. Phil may very well be a genetic anomaly, if you will. A simple product of 'hobosynthesis'."

"*Hobosynthesis?*" Sean spat, barely containing his chug of beer through a fit of laughter. "Now you're just making shit up."

"Oh, no," said Tiv firmly, defending his stance. "The latest journal of *Shithouse Science* supports this theory. After years of exhaustive research into the history and behavior of unrelated hobos, a group of intrepid scientists recently uncovered the elusive "bum" gene. It was just kind of laying there in the middle of all the other genes, not doing anything, leaving all that other important shit like making brain cells to everybody else. They suspect all the lazy fuckers of the world came from the same original hobo from millions of years ago."

Sean laughed and pulled another long swig from his beer. He knew Tiv was on a roll and it would only get better, which meant trouble for poor Phil. Tiv knew he had them for good once Petey Hogan popped a raucous beer fart sending the others into tears of laughter. Not even Jimmy could stop him now.

"Oh, yes," he confirmed with a nod of his head. "It's true. When the penultimate lungfish crawled out of the primordial soup, he turned to the last one left behind and said, 'Come on. Through millions of years of struggle and adaptation, we will one day rule the food chain.' That legless little shit just sat there at the edge of the new world order on his little flipper-elbows and said... 'Nah. I'll just hang around here and see what happens.'"

Sean had to place his glass down out of fear of dropping it; Petey did his best to hold in another nasty beer blast. Even Jimmy B. was fighting to hold back a burst of chuckles.

"Are you implying that evolution has somehow passed Phillie by?" posed Sean, carefully wording his comment to bait Tiv. Phil gave him an *Et tu, Brute'?* glance, but Sean just followed through with a shrug and point at Tiv in an "it's not me, it's him" gesture - a feeble attempt to disguise his own jump onto the bandwagon of roasting their friend. "Maybe he's happy in the soup?" continued Sean, placing a hand of support on Phil's shoulder.

"Maybe, maybe...," offered Tiv, employing strategic pauses, "but one thing I'm sure of... that last lungfish... that lazy little mud-fucker," he drew a pointed finger in Phil's direction, "was Phil's great-great-great-great grandfather."

The laughter burst forth so loudly it was hard to tell which laughs came from who. Even Jimmy B. contributed a hearty outburst.

Phil lifted his glass in a silent mock toast to Tiv. He knew there was no good to come of letting Tiv get under his skin. It was just his turn in the barrel. He decided to ride it out. Mercifully, it didn't last much longer.

The door to Jimmy B.'s opened and closed with a pull that sucked the air from the room. A visibly upset young woman entered the bar and huddled just inside the door for a moment before collecting herself and looking around the room. She glanced quickly over the group, sparing an extra second on Tiv before dropping her eyes back into a tense bounce. She made no motion toward anyone else or even toward the bar. She found a seat at one of the small tables against the wall and sat slowly down and began rummaging nervously in her purse.

"Check it out," Sean said, tapping Tiv's elbow. "Maria Fusco."

Tiv didn't bother turning. He had spotted her as she came in. "She's coming into her own these days, huh?" His words carried a hint of appetite.

"Oh, shit Tiv. Come on. You're not working her are you?" Sean said with mock aversion. "That's more trouble than even *you* can handle."

"Yeah," he conceded. "I knew she was nuts when she showed me her tits back in sixth grade," Tiv said retrospectively.

"She showed you her tits?" Pete spat out, nearly choking on a chug of beer.

"Some guys just walk in the light, Petey," said Sean, clapping Tiv on the shoulder.

"Were they any good?" Pete asked unashamedly.

"She was eleven, you fucking freak!" Tiv slapped the back of Pete's head. "You're right though, Sean. I do like trouble, but that's the Kiss of Death."

Just then, the door opened once again and a young

man entered.

"Hey, Matt's here," Sean said. "MATTY," he beckoned from the back of the bar. Matt Harrington looked back at the sound of his name and he waved and nodded without even realizing who had called out to him, then conspicuously scanned the room, trying to pull shapes from the dim light. He spotted his quarry at the small table to his right and made for the chair that held the girl who had entered just before him. She jolted in her seat as he put his hand on her shoulder and squatted down next to her.

"Well I guess we better plan a funeral 'cause it looks like our boy Matty is a dead man."

Tiv spun at this and spied out the two figures at the table. "No way! What the fuck is he thinking? I know things have been dry for him lately, but this is suicide. Come on," he said, tapping Sean's chest with the back of his hand, "We've got to save him."

Tiv's rescue plan didn't have time to get off the ground. As he and Sean moved toward their friend, his conversation with the girl ended abruptly with her screaming "FUCK YOU!" in his face and making as hasty an exit as she had an entrance.

Matty Harrington was still in a squat position beside the now empty table as his friends approached. He stayed that way for another few moments then rose slowly like a boxer fighting a standing eight count.

"Hey, Matty. What was that?" Sean asked with a chuckle.

"That's some crazy bitch, right there, man. Let that shit go," Tiv contributed. "Come on, Romeo Reject, belly up to the bar." Tiv clutched him by the shoulder and nudged him toward their spot at the bar. "Jimmy," he called out as they approached, drawing the man's attention and pointing to Matty as they neared. The beer was already waiting.

"So what *was* that, Matty?" Tiv asked.

"Agh," Matty grunted, as if he just wanted to shrug it off and forget it. "Nothing."

"Nothing my ass, Matty," Sean said. "*Maria Fusco?* Come on, man. Own up."

Matty pulled a long draw from his glass and looked over at Sean with a slightly surrendered - but still pissed-off - face.

"I was just asking her about her brother, Pino. I heard about a job down at the building I'm working in. They're looking for porters and janitors, stuff like that. I know they hire people with...disabilities, you know."

"Pino the Retard?" Pete chimed in. Matty's shoulders tightened at Pete's reference.

"Fuck you, Pete," Matty said, with a conspicuous amount of contempt. "The guy's not retarded, he's epileptic."

"Well fuck you too, Matt. If I remember correctly, it was you who first called him 'Pino the Retard'," Pete shot back.

"Yeah, well that was a long time ago, and it was a mistake," Matty returned, now with an equally conspicuous amount of introspection. Pete obviously wasn't the source of Matty's ire; he was merely the dupe on hand. "The guy's just had a fucked up life, that's all."

"Yeah, so," Pete hammered back. "What am I living the Life of Riley?"

Matt wasn't so quick to answer. He sipped his beer and let some unspoken thought move across his face like a window shade rolling up and down.

"You could have it worse," he murmured.

"Man, what is with you?" Sean asked.

"I'm just saying that all that 'retard' shit wasn't right. It wasn't his fault, you know. He had those fits and instead of helping the kid out, his parents were embarrassed and took it out on him. The guy's old man used to beat the shit out of him all the time. You've seen it. Right on the fucking street." Matt pulled from his beer, his tone dropping back to a thought spoken aloud. "You can't beat something like that out of somebody."

"That's that 'old country' shit," Tiv interjected. "Fucked up kids were like a mark on the family. A disgrace, especially if it was the son. Pino's old man probably couldn't handle the shame, man. That's life, Matty," Tiv said. "My grandmother was like that. She was an old country Sicilian. She told me stories about people throwing little freak babies off of cliffs into the ocean for being born with a hare lip." Tiv pumped up his chest with pride, half-kidding, but secretly boasting, "That's why the old witch loved me. Good genes."

"Here we go with the genes again," Sean said, laughing.

"Well, we only made it worse for the poor bastard," Matt said.

"Easy on the 'we', white man. Don't go apologizing for me," Tiv said. "I have a strict 'no regrets' policy. Life *is* what it *is*. People like Pino – as tragic as their lives may be – are essential to society. Without them, everybody would be the same. The world makes them because the world needs them. It's simple social stratification. Every culture has it. "

"*Stratification*!" Sean nearly leaped in reaction to his friend's increasingly academic assessments of the neighborhood crowd previously known as 'shit heads and assholes', not to mention 'retards'. "I see your 'stratification' and raise you one 'bullshit'," Sean said.

"It's just culling the herd.," Tiv continued. "The natural order of things."

"Boy, you're a real progressive thinker there Tiv," Sean responded. "If everybody got the same breaks, they wouldn't really be breaks? Is that the theory?"

"Maybe *your* theory. I subscribe to the 'you make your own breaks' school of thought."

"You know, maybe some people just need that one chance to give themselves some sense of being able to actually make it. You can't concede one little victory?" Sean asked.

"That's just prolonging the pain. Things just aren't the same for everybody – plain and simple and painfully true, but true none the less."

"And that's it? Give it up now because you *is* what you *is?*'

"People don't want to put in the effort to improve themselves, Sean." He offered a nod in poor Phil's direction for humorous emphasis. "They just want to walk in comfortable shoes."

The thrust of the conversation began to make Matt writhe inside himself.

"You gotta' have a clear understanding of the world around you, my friend, otherwise you're just pissing in the wind,"

"Uh-oh. Now you're '*my friend*'-ing me. That's a clear signal to end this conversation," Sean said, sensing the mood of the casual night drifting toward uncomfortable waters. Matt picked up on this as well and stepped back from the bar, leaving a five dollar bill in his place.

"I'm taking off," he said, clapping Sean on the shoulder,

"Matty, where you going?" Sean asked. Matt just shrugged his shoulders as he pulled open the door and got eaten by the night.

Tiv shook his head and called after him, "Don't chase that ass, Matty. There's no pussy in the world worth your piece of mind."

"Speak for yourself, Tiv. I'd give up some brains for a shot at Maria, crazy and all," Petey said.

"There's a small sacrifice!" Tiv remarked, his trademark wicked grin returning to his face as he prepared to skewer his hapless friend.

Well, that went well.

Matt found himself back out on the street, not sure which way to go. There was no sign of Maria, not that he wanted to face her again.

How the hell did this night get away from me?

Matty Harrington had emerged into the night barely an hour before like a stone dropped in mud. The walls of his room had begun to press in around him and he needed to get out. An unrest had been stirring in his chest for a while and he had been trying to ignore it, but it was starting to gnaw. It had started slow, coming in tiny teasing moments of clarity, glimpses of light through dirty windows. Possibility was playing peek-a-boo with his soul, and reeking havoc on his heart. He had suddenly found himself sharing the blissful ignorance that he had spent his life polishing with an unfamiliar intimation different than the simple desires that had confronted his youth: the desire for friends, the desire for possessions, and the desire for sex. This new feeling was an alien desire that wasn't so easily recognized, or welcome. It was the desire for change, the need to move ahead, to move on with his life toward something more than what his childhood had offered. He began to see all the people of his young life in the harsh light of sudden truth. The kind of truth that pushes aside well-worn memories and allegiances, that wipes the slate clean without regard to kinship or friendship. The truth that too often spills from the mouths of bitter people that always begins with "let me tell you..." and makes you want to smash their ugly faces with your fists. Foreign, unwelcome truth. He hated it.

He stepped into the grisaille effigy of a neighborhood, moving aimlessly past quiet houses that he had walked by a thousand times in his life, offering nothing but their facades. People's lives were inches away, yet he knew nothing that went on behind the closed doors and shaded windows. Women would whisper and stories would fly, none of it reliable, but almost always branded as truth. People served up stories of infidelity and shame and others happily feasted on them like poisoned pastries.

The growing feeling of being out of place stole his confidence from him. It was like he suddenly saw the streets outside differently, something suddenly unfamiliar and all too familiar at the same time. Something uncomfortable.

Unfocused and detached, Matt had walked until he found himself approaching the quiet, fenced-in patch of Bronx real estate that could only be referred to as a "park" in urbania. Just a few years ago, the worn, green-painted, wooden slat benches would have been lined with Matt and his friends, but they were now empty. No more gatherings of restless youths swarming like moths around the street lamps that ringed the park. Matt, Sean, Tiv, all of them, were apparently the end of the line.

Fucking remnants. That's what we've become.

Out of sheer habit, Matt sat on the second bench. The kids of the neighborhood had been following park protocol forever. Each separate group of kids had their own benches, mostly designated by age, though some allowances were made on nights when fewer kids were hanging out, but generally, here at the park, rules were tacitly self-enforced. Matty's group had the second bench. First bench – closest to the corner and most visible – was always for the oldest kids. Though Matty was among the elders now, the second bench was where he felt he belonged. Jimmy B. was an original first-bencher, as was Matty's brother Jackie, at least until Jimmy took over the Emerald, moving most of the first-benchers onto barstools.

Five nights a week on a stool in Jimmy's – that's what it all amounts to, huh? One long memory, except we all get older and more pathetic each time we think about it. What was that story about the guy with the aging picture? Mr. Gray or Dr. Gray or some shit like that. That's what it is. Memories like that fucking picture, only in reverse.

And with that moment of clarity came a cloud of guilt and feeling of treason...

So am I just going to discount every person I know just because I want to leave everything behind?

His own duplicity was an unwelcome intruder in his silent lucidity.

I know this is where I grew up, but once the growing up is done, you've got to take the next step. Keep growing. I can't do it here. I don't want this place to wring any more out of me. I don't want to be some forgotten straggler wandering around here wondering where the hell my life went."

Matty was certain that he was sitting on the tail of Ouroboros waiting to be swallowed and he had had enough. The only way ahead was to leave the neighborhood behind. He wanted out of The Bronx.

Matt sat at the edge of the shadow play that existed even in the deepening night, though there were probably more shades than shadows. The benches were empty but even so, no one ever sat alone. The park was one of the few places were a person could come and sit with ghosts of people who weren't even dead. They were all there: Minks: the left-over junkie from the Sixties whose lips were once nearly blown off by a firecracker wrapped in rolling paper left by Joey Patone under the park bench just to see if Minks would smoke it; Arnie: the guitar-playing hippie detritus of Jimmy B.'s crew who taught just about every kid in the neighborhood how to play *All Along the Watchtower* on the guitar whether they wanted to know it or not; Brow: the little Puerto Rican kid with the birthmark on his forehead that resembled a third eyebrow, who worked in Benny's bodega out of which he came running one night screaming "Benny got shot! Benny got shot!" when in fact Benny had been shot as three guys robbed the shitty little store one Friday evening – Benny died.

But nowhere among the shadows was Pino Fusco. Pino wasn't allowed on the benches. As a kid, he could play in the park - use the swings, the slide - but come dusk, when the real boys came out to play, Pino was gone. Even as stunted as he may have been, he understood being the object of ridicule from an early age, learning at the brutal end of the stick of youthful torment. Pino the Retard, Pino the Elastic Spastic, Freaky Fusco, and every other combination of words that would fit at the time. His miserable past didn't even rate a ghost, nor did it require a rumor. There was no need for creative gossip in Pino's case.

Pino's father, Ciro, put it all out there on the street. The drunken beatings, the berating, the belittling. It was a damn opera without the fat lady. He wrote the script for every tormentor to follow. *My son is a disgrace, do with him as you will.* He might as well just have said it outright, broken English and all.

The crazy, cruel old man left it all there for kids like Matty and the rest to lap up and spit back out at Pino.

And they did with a vengeance.

Never was there a more brutalized being in this neighborhood of dog-eat-dog proclivity. From the first open air seizure on the sidewalk outside St. Dominic's Church after morning mass when he was six, Pino was outed. Moving rapidly in his celebrity from feared to pitied to imitated to mocked, he was doomed, and it seemed as if his father knew this. The old man watched his boy writhe on the hard concrete with the rest of the onlookers as if he were no more than a stricken dog. So a dog it was. The neighborhood mutt.

Matt absentmindedly rubbed his right eye. It was a habit that surfaced without warning, born of an old injury long since healed yet never fully forgotten or forgiven - his reward for a moment of kindness...or weakness. The outcome would come to label the act.

It was a standard lazy summer afternoon, one day back when he was twelve. No one else was around, no one at the park, no one on the corner. No one, but Pino Fusco, sitting alone on a bench. Succumbing to an odd sense of loneliness that he never came to understand as Pino's or his own, Matt made his way over to the lone boy. "You wanna' hit a few," he said as he pulled the always present 'Spaldeen' from his front pocket. Shocked into speechlessness by Matt's unexpected offer, Pino could only muster an awkward nod of his head that Matt at first mistook for the beginnings of a seizure. He retrieved the stick-ball bat that he and his friends kept hidden at the edge of the fence that ringed the park and handed the skinny stick wrapped on one end with black tape to the eager Pino. Matt reached down to mark home plate with a piece of chalk and when he stood back up he was met with the most excruciating and unexpected pain of his young life. Pino, swinging wildly, obviously elated at simply being asked to play, never having had a chance to even learn stick ball etiquette much less practice it, struck Matt with the full force of his excitement - and the blunt end of the bat - right in his eye socket. A more perfect fit of flesh and wood could not have been executed outside the realm of bad luck. It took more than a week for the swelling to release Matt's eye and two more weeks for the bruises to fade. To his credit, Pino did go fetch Matt's mother as he lay curled up on the ground holding his injured eye, but nevertheless, a much more aggressive campaign of torment ensued for the hapless Pino that summer.

That's what Matt got the last time he had the desire to change the established order of things where Pino was concerned: an eyeful of blood and a lifelong tie to a "retard". That's the thing about pain, in all its formless beauty, whether it is physical or emotional, it's not a solitary human element. It is a magnificent unifier. Whether you cause it or you receive it, it bonds the souls of those involved forever.

So Pino Fusco *was* a ghost, after all. He was that piece of unfinished business that haunts the back of your head forever, just waiting to say "BOO" when you're not expecting it. Matt needed to get unstuck from this ghost. That was where the job scenario came into play. Giving Pino a chance to stand on his own, to be treated as a productive part of the world around him instead of the casualty that Matt had contributed to. Maybe an act of atonement could provide some release, some karmic crowbar to pry their fates apart? But how to take the first step? He played a thousand scenarios over in his mind, yet none found their mark. They just grew into one huge stone inside his skull.

Then he saw *her*. Maria Fusco, Pino's sister. Maria

would be the one to cut the stone out.

Matt stood up from the bench, sending the shades scampering back to the shadows.

"Hey, Maria. Hey, wait up."

The figure ahead of him cut an erratic swath down the street. Maria was all swinging hips barely controlling mercurial legs that seemed to work at double speed, dark hair that fluttered in flame-like silhouette engulfing a lolling head that somehow maintained a forward motivation. Tight clothes struggled to contain her determined body with each demanding step. At Matt's hail, she shot a glance over her shoulder. Her momentum wouldn't allow any unscheduled change in course. After a few steps she reigned herself to a stop and offered a second glance back. A single wide, dark eye peered out from behind the untamed hair that somehow continued to flutter on a windless night.

Had Matty been close enough to meet that stare, he may have abandoned his plan and slipped back into the night. Blinded by his own agenda, he approached her.

At first sight, Maria Fusco was seemingly attractive. Her face was pretty with large eyes and full lips, framed by a mane of dark hair that moved with a life of its own; her body was womanly in a way that hinted that she probably had developed at a young age. Full breasts thrust their cleavage up as a challenge for anyone to try and ignore their presence as her shoulders pulled back to redouble the dare. She insinuated danger and that was where the bait and switch took place. She *was* dangerous, but not the kind that should have lured men beyond hope of rational thinking, but instead she was fearsome in a way that advised you to stay back. She emitted a feral femininity that was more terrifying than inviting. Her sexuality didn't promise intimacy, it intimated umbrage.

"Hey, where you going?"

"What?"

Her voice was a mix of confusion and mistrust. What the hell could Matty Harrington want with her? She stayed with her feet still pointed in the direction she was headed. She talked to him off her shoulder like a disinterested bystander.

"Where're you going? I was just hanging at the park and I saw you tearing by in a hurry." It was funny how hard it became to talk *to* someone who he had no trouble talking *about* for years.

"I was just going to hook up with Gina. We're going up to Yonkers later."

"Yonkers? What's up there?" Matt's feigned charm barely made it past his vulnerability.

"There's a new club on Central Avenue that opened a few weeks ago. Gina says it's good." Maria eyed Matt up and down through wary eyes. Matt was one of many neighborhood guys she had included on her 'do-able' list of potential lovers a while back. He never gave her the time of day all through their teen years, but she made allowances. "You wanna' come? Gina' wouldn't mind."

"Nah. I'm not up for a crowded place."

Maria's eyes narrowed slightly. Was Matty Harrington hitting on her? He's pretty crude if he was. Still, she hadn't crossed him off the list yet. She turned to face him and her breasts offered up their full frontal assault.

"So what, you're gonna' hang out at an empty park?"

"It's nice when it's quiet around here for a change. I can think better."

"Yeah? What do you think about here in the dark by yourself?" She moved just a bit closer.

"Everything and nothing. This neighborhood."

"Do yourself a favor and stop thinking. There's no place for philosophers in The Bronx, Matty, only assholes who think they know better than everyone else. You spend too much time thinking about this place and you'll realize what a shithole you're stuck in." She reached over and grabbed his elbow. "Come on, you obviously need to get away from here for awhile."

Matt heard Maria, but he didn't listen. Plans were

already in play in his head and he had no interest or intention to stray from them. He played along, having every intention of pulling out at the last minute.

"Yeah, maybe," he said, letting Maria tug him along by the arm. "So Gina, huh? I haven't seen her in awhile. You guys still friends? I remember some pretty good blow-ups between you two." He was reaching with his lame attempt at small talk. She appeared not to notice.

"She can be a bitch, but she's still one of the only people around here who knows how to have fun."

Matt found himself in near-double time keeping up with Maria's pace. With his pulse already kicked up, he decided to make his move.

"So how's your brother, Pino? I haven't seen him around lately."

In the subtle way that a growing electrical charge slowly causes muscles to twitch before seizing, he could feel a tingle move from Maria's hand to his arm. He wasn't sure if it was a trickle of anger or surprise or some other unseen force, but it seemed as if the mention of Pino's name caused an immediate reaction in Maria. No response, only reaction. One that Matty foolishly chose to ignore.

"Is he working or anything?"

Maria hit the brakes and spun on Matt . There was no tingle coming from her now. It was the full on zap of a screwdriver in an electrical socket. The unexpected surge paralyzed him.

"What the fuck do you care about my brother?" Any air of invitation that she had offered up a moment ago had retreated behind a wall of distrust.

Dumbfounded in the face of a confrontation he never anticipated, Matt floundered. "I don't...I was just asking."

Maria let go of his arm and squared off in front of him. Her small size grew in proportion to her rage. She eyed him through her tendrils of living hair, but said nothing. Matt was being commanded to talk by the bristling dark figure before him - her silence pressing into him as if trying to push his words out, her lips parting into La Bocca della Verita, daring him to lie to her so she could bite off his hands.

"I heard about some jobs down where I work...I thought..."

"You thought what? You don't know anything about my family, so mind your own fucking business."

Maria spun back around and took off as if she had never stopped. She had one pace – full on.

Shit!

Matt watched her shape move away in an otherworldly glow of fury that seemed to push aside the night. Without a clear thought anymore, he began to follow her. She must have sensed him behind her because she made a quick left into Jimmy B.'s. He hesitated at following her into the Emerald. He was barely able to deal with Maria, he dreaded the idea of having to add anybody else to the mix. Reluctantly, he pulled open the door and entered Jimmy B.'s Emerald Bar. The last thing he wanted was an audience. Yet that was exactly what he got.

Standing outside the Emerald in the aftershock of Maria Fusco, Matty was still shaken by her reaction. *Why the hell did she go off the handle? Crazy bitch. Like father, like daughter. This poor bastard Pino gets it from all ends.* The thought just made the stone in his head that much heavier.

Heading back toward the park seemed like an empty option now, and there was nothing behind him in The Emerald but the mindless chattering of his friends. Walking out on them only emboldened his new-found detachment. *Who's the remnant now, asshole*, he chided himself. If the streets that had raised him no longer included him, that didn't make them something different, it made *him* something different.

Which is what? Part of Tiv's herd? Fuck him.

He took a few steps in no direction and sucked in a slow breath of subordination. It looked like Pino's ghost would be with him a little while longer

.

§

Maria Fusco took off from the Emerald in a fit of rage, not mere outrage at Matty's deceit, but deep rage at his pity. *Pino. Pino. They made a fool of him for years, a neighborhood joke, and now they feel bad for him. For HIM! They think I don't know all the names they had for me too. They think I don't know how they look at me. But they feel sorry for HIM! They should only know what a monster he is. God gave him his disease for a reason.*

Her direction didn't matter; all that mattered was that she kept moving. Maria was a force of perpetual motion. Filling her with anger only urged her to greater speeds. The clap of her heels against the hard concrete of the sidewalk made the sound of muffled gunshots and she was quickly reaching Tommy Gun levels.

"Son of a bitch! Who the fuck does he think he is?" Her voice smoldered and chopped the words. "He should only know. They should all know." She knew that would never happen. No one would ever know about Pino. No one but her...and her father.

Maria's engine of fury pumped her legs like pistons and churned her heart until it reached a point of saturation, at which she abruptly stomped to a halt. The only release for her frustration and anger would now be through her mouth. She needed to hear it in her ears, no longer satisfied by the screams in her head. It manifested itself in the usual all-encompassing, one-size-fits-all, universal declaration of outrage, the great equalizer - "FUCK!"

She threw her hands up in the air and let the fire pour out of her chest. Her long nails stabbed at the sky like daggers before clenching into tight fists. She let her primal cry escape once more. This time, the resounding "FUCK" bounced back at her in a deep echo.

Without realizing, her walking rage had led her to the steps of St. Dominic's. It was the dark, cavernous portico of the old church that had swallowed her harsh words and sent them back to her in a bellow of admonition. Darkness shrouded the raised entryway and a worn carpet rolled down the wide concrete steps like an old man's tongue. It was as if God himself had opened his mouth to voice his disapproval of her vulgarity in front of his solemn place. Her anger waned and shame began to crawl over her skin. All of her years of Catholic school and Sunday Mass had instilled this need for humility in her, for submission, for forgiveness. Where Irish Catholics were made pious through guilt, Italians were made so through shame. Her mother would be vilified by her friends for Maria's behavior in front of the church, the place of God, and her father...her father. At the thought of him her anger surged back and cast aside the weaker emotion of shame. She would be glad if she could shame her father. He brought more shame in silence upon himself and his family than any words of hers could ever bring.

"FUCK YOU," she shouted at God's mouth, daring the words to come back to her. "YOU MADE HIM. YOU MADE THAT FUCKING MONSTER."

Maria's words pulled at her insides as she heaved them out. She wanted them to rip the source of her bile from her soul, to finally rid herself of the loathing that lived there, but no amount of screaming or swearing or foot stomping and finger clutching would do that for her. Her animus was pressed too deep into the flesh of her body years ago by the monster's hungry fingers, the horror of his unnatural lust crudely guiding his callous hands over her prematurely pubescent breasts, groping her defenseless virtue. Rough, thoughtless vile fingers, probing and defiling that which he should have been protecting. The disregard for the innocence of that ten year old girl would lay the groundwork for the terminal chaos of her heart. Brothers should be guardians not betrayers.

And neither should father's.

He knew. I could see it in his eyes even then. He knew and he left me on my own. A little girl, A LITTLE FUCKING GIRL! A virginal sacrifice to redeem his broken boy. I know he was right outside that door every time, but he never stopped it. I stopped it, not him. I stopped his fucking son.

Her fingers writhed with their own memories. The feeling of grasping and tearing, the feeling of the warm blood filling her palm and the rent flesh squirming as she crushed the life from the olive-shaped appendages. He would never molest her again. He would never molest anyone.

"I STOPPED HIM! NOT EVEN YOU COULD DO IT! I DID IT" This time the words did echo back at her.

She ended her tirade as it had began, with a long shameless, "FUUCCKK!"

"Maria," came the call. At first it didn't register in her ears, which were still ringing from her own screams.

"Maria!" This time she heard and turned to find Gina staring at her from the window of a car that had pulled up alongside the curb behind her.

"What are you doing?" Gina said, with a somewhat bewildered, but apprehensive, look on her face. "I've been looking all over for you. I thought we were going out?"

Maria turned her back on the church and headed for the car. She nearly yanked the door handle off as she got in.

"Let's get out of here. I swear I hate this damn place."

.

SCARECROW

The phone rang just as Kevin was opening the door. He stepped inside and nudged the door closed with his foot. He slipped his jacket onto its hook, pulled the heavy work boots off his tired feet and dropped them by the door. With an almost whimpering flutter, the phone rang again. He hated the annoying electronic sound that the phone made when it "rang". No more clanging bells like the phone in his house when he was a kid. That old wall phone rang like it meant something. The jarring clash of bells demanded your attention and compelled you to answer. It was a call to arms. Now, a telephone's "ringer" was just an intrusive buzz heralding yet another pointless call heading for the answering machine.

They took the damn balls out of the telephone, he thought.

"Ann Marie," he called out. "You here? You gonna' get that, baby?"

She didn't answer his beckoning, or the phone's.

He headed for the kitchen, which is where his wife usually was around this time, making some kind of late dinner for him.

It was Monday. Monday was a late overtime day for Kevin. *Could be worse,* he often thought of having to work late on the first night after the weekend. *They could make us do it on Sundays instead.*

He stuck his head in the kitchen doorway and found Ann Marie. There was no dinner waiting there for him, only Ann Marie and an empty table. She was puffing angrily on a cigarette, and sitting on one of the little chairs that she had bought last year when she decided to refurnish the kitchen in a Fifties-retro theme. He hated the little chrome chairs with the bright red seats. He said they made him feel like he was a reject from *Happy Days*. She said he was an asshole.

Oh, shit, he thought. *What now?*

There was a heavy green glass ashtray full of dead butts on the table next to her. It clashed mightily with the bright red and chrome of the table. Her legs were crossed in an impatient way, one of them bouncing hard against the other.

Ann Marie was a small girl, but when she wasn't happy, she was the proverbial 800lb. gorilla. One with a bad attitude.

"Ann Marie, baby," he said, pretending not to pick up on her conspicuous anger, hoping against instinct that he could duck the punch. "You gonna' get that, or should I just let it go to the machine?"

She waited a second before she shot him a look that could stop a charging bull. Her face wore a *fuck you* better than anybody Kevin had ever met.

The castrated phone fluttered on.

"Well I'm not gonna' get it. It's probably Gina. It's always Gina. You guys might as well just get two cups and a string. I mean, she lives right across the street. Or, how about them new walkie-talkies...sorry, "personal communication devices", everybody's getting now. 'Breaker breaker, come in Gina this is Ann Marie, over. Doctor Dickhead just slept with his sister on 'One Life to Lose', over."

Ann Marie wasn't responding well to Kevin's humor.

"Why don't you get it," she said flatly, with enough acid in her voice to melt the wax in Kevin's ears. "It's for you anyway."

Here it comes.

"What do you mean?" he said.

"I'm sure it's that bitch again."

Bingo!

"What 'bitch' would that be? Has my mother been trying to call? What if it's something important? You know my father's heart has been acting up again."

"Wrong bitch, Kevin. And, there's nothing wrong with your father's heart. He just wishes there was so he could escape your mother. No, Kevin…try, Christine."

Christine?

"Christine who?"

"Christine the *bitch* who lives in the big house in Country Club. You know, the one who snagged the only worthwhile one of your lazy bastard friends." Ann Marie's voice twisted slightly and her eyes moved wickedly into their corners. "You know, Kevin, Anthony always had his eyes on my ass, but noooo, I was *your* girlfriend. I could never do that to you. I would have had to be 'crazy', all my friends said. *Kevin is soooo cute.* Anyway, I was just a little bit late. Christine came along and must have just spread a little quicker."

"Who's the bitch now, Ann Marie?"

"Oh, *I'm* a bitch? You know what Kevin - fuck you."

"You know, Ann Marie, if you have nothing nice to say, then just don't say anything." All the humor had drained from his body. *Now I get it. Christine must have called today. What could she want?*

Ann Marie hated Christine Mazur from the first moment Anthony Gagliardi brought her to the neighborhood. Kevin and Ann Marie and their friends were a neighborhood bunch that had been together since elementary school. Most of the kids in the close knit Bronx neighborhood all went to the same parochial school, St. Dominic's, and even the same high school, St. Raymond's in Castle Hill. They were the archetypal neighborhood kids -

they played together, they grew up together, and they found out about life, and with Kevin and Ann Marie, even love, together. As they grew out of their teens, they grew into adulthood together. They were bridesmaids and maids of honor, ushers and best men at each other's weddings, and even more recently, godparents to each other's children. Christine Mazur wasn't part of that mix. Anthony met her at a bar in Eastchester. She was a "spoiled little rich bitch", according to Ann Marie and her friends. It was part jealousy, and part fact. Ann Marie and the girls made no attempt to make her feel comfortable when they all got together, and Christine responded in kind. She made sure they all knew about her huge house in the suburbs – a point not lost on kids used to narrow Bronx houses and postage stamp backyards.

Then there was Anthony.

Anthony Gagliardi was long regarded as one of the best looking guys in the neighborhood, and Christine got him. An outsider, a stranger, got the best guy in the bunch. That broke Gina's heart. Gina Gaetti, Ann Marie's best friend, had been in love with Anthony since she was a little girl. They were a couple off and on throughout their teens, and then suddenly, just as everybody seemed to be settling down - Kevin and Ann Marie were already engaged - Anthony showed up with Christine. Gina was crushed, and as her best friend, Ann Marie was obliged to hate Christine forever, a feat she accomplished with great success.

Kevin always felt bad about that. He and Anthony were as close as two friends could get, and not being able to move forward into the next phase of their lives with the same ease and familiarity as their childhood bothered him. He didn't hold it against Ann Marie, but he secretly wished she would some day move past it.

Beside it all, he liked Christine. She was the perfect match for his friend. She calmed his rowdy ways, and gave him focus. Anthony had learned the tile mason's trade from his father and went right to work out of high school. He did well - he was always the one with a pocketful of money - but when he and Christine got married, they built Anthony's skill into a successful business. Kevin always felt they viewed their marriage as a team, and that was what he hoped for with Ann Marie, but it never seemed to happen. Ann Marie stopped working about a year after they got married so she could finish college. Kevin had been working as an HVAC mechanic since he graduated from high school, and the money seemed to be pretty good, so they decided it was a worthwhile move, but after two semesters, Ann Marie quit. At first, she said she didn't like the school, then it was the professors, then the other students. She said she didn't fit in. College life wasn't for her. That was eight years ago, and she never went back to school, or work. *"We'll start a family",* was her next phase, but after two years of trying, she still couldn't get pregnant. The team spirit kind of withered for Kevin and Ann Marie.

Kevin didn't regret his choices; he truly loved Ann Marie, but sometimes secretly wished that his life could have turned out more like Anthony's.

He reached for the phone on the kitchen wall.

"Hello."

"Hello, Kevin?" It *was* Christine. Her voice was instantly recognizable to him. It was void of the trademark "Bronxisms" that you only notice in their absence.

"Yeah. Hi, Christine?"

"Yes."

"Hi. How are you doing?" He could barely hide a wince as Ann Marie's foot began to rock harder and faster. The cigarette in her mouth seemed to have the life sucked out of it with a single angry drag. He turned to avoid her eyes; he knew what they were doing, he could feel their heat now on the back of his head.

"Well, uh, Kevin...I hate to bother you. When I called before, Ann Marie told me you were still at work, and I feel awful about calling you with this now...but I didn't know who else to call."

Her voice quivered as if she was trying to hold back tears.

"No, no. It's okay. Really. I just walked in and Ann Marie and I were going to have a late dinner, and as it turns out it going to be a little later than we thought."

Ann Marie pounded the dead cigarette butt into the ashtray until it was nothing more than a crumpled brown ball of cotton. She pulled another from the pack on the table and lit it with a fierce draw. She sent an angry smoke signal in Kevin's direction.

"What is it? Is everything okay?" he asked.

"Well…it's Anthony. Something's going on, and I'm starting to get scared."

Kevin's face drew in with concern. *Anthony? What the hell could be wrong with Anthony?*

"What is it? Is he sick?"

"No, no. It's just…"

Her voice broke and Kevin could hear her trying to collect herself on the other end of the phone.

"Something's wrong with him. I've never seen him like this. Everything's been great…but last Thursday, he left early in the morning, then he called me after lunch and said he was going out to estimate a job and that he would be home around five. When he hadn't come home by seven, I had already paged him five times. I tried the cell phone, I tried everything, but I just couldn't reach him. By midnight I was ready to call the police, but then about an hour later, he came home. You know him, Kevin. He's not that type. He doesn't just go out after work and not tell me. He doesn't just disappear and not call."

"What did he say when he got home?"

"Well, I asked him what happened, and he wouldn't answer me. He just went into the bedroom, fell onto the bed and stared up at the ceiling. And his eyes, Kevin. That's the scary thing. His eyes looked like he hadn't blinked in days."

Sounds like a coke binge. I'm not going to tell Christine that, but Anthony using drugs? It doesn't make any sense.

"What did he say the next day?"

"That's just it. He wasn't there the next day. He must have gotten up early, or maybe he never even went to sleep, I don't know. He was just gone. He left me a note that said he had something to take care of."

Kevin was just as much at a loss as Christine was. She was right. He wasn't the type to disappear like that, at least not since he met Christine. Anthony was always a little crazier than the rest of the bunch, always the one to take things a step too far, but since Christine, he was steady as a rock. As for drugs, he was no worse than the rest. They all smoked a little weed back then, maybe even a little coke, but never anything like she was describing.

"Is everything all right with you guys?" It was a question that he didn't want to ask, but he had nothing left.

"Yeah. Everything is fine."

"How about the business?"

"Well, business is great."

Kevin knew Christine was the brain behind the business. She handled all the money and the accounts. Anthony handled all the contracting and labor. Big City Tile had become a major player in the local tile business with a new showroom on Tremont Avenue and a warehouse down off of Bruckner. Anthony and Christine were set up pretty good. They had bought a real nice place over in Country Club, the more elite section of the North Bronx. That didn't do much to endear her to Ann Marie. She felt that Christine was just flaunting it in everyone's faces.

"This isn't about us, or the business, Kevin. This is something of his. That's why I thought you might know?"

"Geez. Christine. I'm at a loss. Do you know where he is now? Maybe I could talk to him and find out what this is all about."

Ann Marie's feet uncrossed and hit the floor hard. She moved over to the kitchen sink, turned on the faucet full blast and pounded her latest Marlboro victim into the white enamel. It sizzled as it died, but paled next to the fire that was smoldering in Ann Marie's eyes.

Kevin turned away from the vision of his angry wife. His concern had started to turn from curiosity to alarm. *Something is going on, but what the hell could it be about?*

"Is there anything else that might explain this?"

Christine hesitated on the line. He could tell there was one more thing coming.

"Well…there is some money gone. It was withdrawn this morning from our personal account."

Money?

"How much money, Christine?"

She hesitated again.

"All of it. Our entire savings account. Over eighty-five thousand dollars."

Kevin's voice jumped out before Christine had even finished talking.

"*WHAT!* Eighty-five thousand! What the hell is he doing on the street with that kind of money?"

He had spoken before he had a chance to think, and now he thought the better of his outburst. Ann Marie had a sudden interest in the conversation now, and she waited with a Cheshire cat grin for her husband to finish his phone call. She would have plenty to say now, and *"Sorry, Kevin"*; none of it would be nice.

Shit! I shouldn't have done that.

"I'm sorry, Christine. It's just that that's a lot of money. Wow! He doesn't owe any money on the street, does he?" He was more thinking aloud to himself than asking Christine.

"I…don't know. I don't know anything about that kind of stuff. It couldn't be for the business, all accounts are current. There's nothing wrong there." Her voice was quivering again.

Anthony's never gone to the street before. He's never been into a bookie either. Shit. I know this guy. There's no way he could be going down that hard, is there?

He began to scan his head for anybody or anything that might help him get a handle on this. One name came to him - *Jimmy*!

If Anthony was into anybody around the neighborhood, Jimmy B. would know.

He would go and see Jimmy Burke over at the Emerald. Jimmy was always the "go to" guy, and now Kevin needed him.

"You know what, Christine. Give me a couple hours. I've got a few things that I can look into and then I'll call you back. We'll figure this out, don't worry. Okay?"

She was clearly crying on the other end of the phone. "Thank you, Kevin. I knew you would be the one to help. I'm sorry for calling, but I…"

"Christine, don't worry about it. We'll get it straightened out. We will."

"…okay. Thank you, Kevin."

"Alright. Go relax, it'll be fine."

The phone hung up on the other end long before Kevin put the receiver back in its cradle on the wall. He knew what he would be facing when he turned around toward Ann Marie. She didn't disappoint him

Trouble in Paradise?" Anne Marie's sarcasm would only be outdone by her raw anger.

"Something's going on with Anthony."

"So I heard. He split with the bank account, huh? Well it's good to see he finally wised up and dropped that bitch…oh, sorry to insult your little friend, Kevin. I forgot, I'm the bitch. "

"Come on, Ann Marie. This isn't like the guy. He wouldn't just drop her like that."

"Oh, no. Gina might disagree with you there, Kevin. He dropped her pretty quickly when the 'perfect woman' came along. Maybe, and I know this might be hard for you to believe, but just maybe Anthony found someone better than Christine."

"That whole Gina thing was more than ten years ago,

for Christ's sake. You people have to grow up and move on."

He knew as soon as the words left his lips that he was wrong to say it. It didn't come out the way he intended, but he was caught between his wife and a hard place.

"You people? Kevin, *you people*? Is that what I am now Kevin?"

For a split second, a look of pained hurt crossed Ann Marie's face. It didn't last long before anger wiped it away.

"You're a bastard."

"I'm sorry, Ann Marie. I didn't mean that, but Gina's got to get over that whole thing. He's long gone. There really wasn't anything there to begin with. She chased him. I mean, shit, she practically threw herself at his feet. How could he not jump on her, she made herself available on call. That whole thing was doomed from the start, and you know that. You should be helping her get over it, not helping her carry a grudge."

"Is that the way it works, Kevin? You just get over somebody and move on?"

Her eyes were filled with hurt again.

"What the hell is going on with you? This is not about Anthony or Christine or Gina. What? Is it your time of the month?"

Stupid, Kevin. Real Stupid. He braced himself again.

"Fuck you, Kevin."

"You know what? I gotta' go. Let me just find out what's going on with Anthony, then I'll come back and we can talk."

Ann Marie was quiet now. This is bad, he thought. She was looking down at the floor; he could tell she was ready to cry. She spoke without looking at him.

"No. You're not going." Her voice was soft and though she wanted it to sound like a demand, it was more of a plea.

"What? Come on, Ann Marie. Be reasonable. The woman's worried about her husband. I'm worried about my friend."

"What about me?"

"This isn't about you, Ann Marie."

"It never is, Kevin. That's the point. With you, it's never about me." Her voice was soft and ripe with tears. "From day one, it was never about me. You never thought anything about dropping me when your friends called. Do you think I liked being left behind all the time when you and Anthony and the rest of your asshole friends disappeared for days at a time? "

"I always came back," he tried feebly.

"Sure. You always did, but then you just did it all over again. I thought that when we got married things would be different, but apparently not. Even now, after all these years, you still choose them over me. You choose her over me."

"Come on, Ann Marie. That's not true. This is different. This isn't about hanging out with my friends. Somebody might be in real trouble."

"Somebody is in real trouble, Kevin."

"Don't do this. Please, don't. Just let me find out what's going on. I'll be right back."

"You know what, Kevin." The tears dried and her voice built back to anger.

"While you're out you might as well go fuck her, because you won't be coming near me anymore. Go ahead, go jump when she calls." She turned her back on him and pulled another Marlboro from the near empty pack on the table.

That was his cue to leave. He could never walk out on Ann Marie's tears, but her anger he could run from. He pulled his old sneakers from the closet, slid them on without undoing the laces, and headed for the door.

"I'll be back soon," he called over his shoulder as he pulled the door closed behind him. Something crashed hard into the door just as it closed.

That ashtray. I gotta' remember to get rid of that thing. One of these days she's gonna' nail me for real.

Kevin stepped up to the big wooden door of the Emerald Bar.

Man, this place never changes.

Before he pulled on the well-worn brass handle, he looked overhead.

Same old clunker of an A/C unit.

The old air conditioner was famous for dripping onto the heads of the patrons as they entered the bar. Though it was early October and the unit wasn't turned on or making its familiar groan, Kevin had been indoctrinated years before and ducking the droplets was now pure instinct.

Old habits die real hard, but not as hard as old Freidrichs, he thought.

He tugged at the heavy door and the barroom came into view. Though Kevin hadn't been to the Emerald in a few years - *Wow, had it been years already?* - it was if he was there just yesterday. He could almost still taste the first beer that Jimmy B. had poured him when he hit legal age, not to mention the few that he might have slipped him before then.

There was a pretty good crowd for a Monday Night, but then Kevin remembered the game – Jets and Miami on Monday Night Football. He looked up at the T.V. screen above the bar. The pre-game was already over.

Shit, I wanted to see that. Well that's the least of my problems tonight.

It took a moment before he spotted Jimmy. He was pouring beer down at the other end of the bar. He scanned the rest of the open room carefully, and aside from an older guy he recognized but never really hung out with sitting at the far end by himself, there were no familiar faces in the crowd; and no sign of Anthony. He was glad. He didn't want to make this a night of reunions.

"Hey, the cat's really dragging 'em in off the streets tonight!" called a booming voice from the end of the bar. Jimmy had spotted Kevin and was heading toward him.

Kevin smiled as he drew in close to the long wooden bar to greet Jimmy.

"Jesus, how are you doing Kevin? You finally thought to come back and see me huh?"

"Hey, Jimmy, how's it going? I see you still got the old groaner hanging over the door there. Is it still pissing on people heads?"

"I don't remember you complaining much on those 100 degree-in-the-shade days when you guys would huddle in here for hours."

"That was a bunch of years ago Jimmy and the old Freddy there was already a hundred years old."

"Grab a stool and we'll toast to another hundred." Jimmy laughed and sent his outstretched hand to meet Kevin. "Sit, sit. Come on. Tell me about that cute wife of yours. How's Ann Marie." Jimmy remembered everybody. Ann Marie's name came to him without a moment's pause.

"She's, uh…good, Jimmy. She's home."

Jimmy slipped right into his big brother mode. Time had no effect on Jimmy Burke. He could make anybody feel as if they had spent everyday of their life with him.

"I've heard that 'she's good' one plenty of times before. You're not being an asshole, are you Kevin?"

Me? An asshole? That's not the first time I've heard that tonight!

"That's not what brings you here is it, 'cause I'll send you right back home? I can handle makin' 'em football widows one night a week, but anything more than that, I don't want on my head." He laughed his disarming laugh again.

"No, Jimmy. Actually I need to talk to you about something, if you've got a minute?"

"Sure, Kevin," he said, his trademark smile and understanding eyes jumping into service. "Grab that booth over near the pay phone, I'll be right over."

Jimmy walked the length of the bar topping off beers as he went. He pulled off his bar apron, came out from behind the bar, and made his way toward the booth where Kevin was waiting. Jimmy B. was a big man, and he was even more imposing when he was out from behind the bar. It was if Jimmy was made specifically for bar life. He had the heart of a bartender and the body of a bouncer. Kevin often joked that Jimmy didn't need pants or shoes because no one ever saw them anyway. Jimmy the talking torso, he called him. Jimmy sat down across from Kevin, and Kevin could see that he had brought his big brother face with him.

""What's going on, kid?" Jimmy didn't disappoint. He was probably the only guy who could call a man "kid" and not seem like he was talking down to him.

"It's Anthony, Jimmy. Something's going on. His wife called my house and she's real worried. She said he started acting strange, then he disappeared, and he cleaned out their bank account. Eighty-five grand, Jimmy!"

"Gagliardi? Wow. That's a lot of cash to be hitting the street with." Jimmy's eyes went wide with the mention of the cash. "What's he doing with all that scratch?" Jimmy asked more of himself than Kevin.

"I don't know. I was wondering if you heard anything, like maybe he was into a shy or something."

"Eighty-five grand. That's a lot of money, Kevin. It doesn't seem like Anthony. He never hit the streets for money before, and the amount of money that would pull that kind of vig is crazy."

"I know, I know," Kevin said, dismissing the idea as quickly as he had before when Christine told him earlier about the missing money. "The only thing I can even come up with is maybe he got into a bookie."

"Not around here. You know I don't let anybody I know go down that hard. I let Dom take the football outta' here, this way I can keep an eye on things. You know there's no way to keep a bookmaker out of the neighborhood. I figure it's best to keep it where I can watch it, so I give Dom some room - at least he's a local."

"I figured Dom would know, but I didn't want to get

too many people involved in this until I have some idea what's going on."

Dominic Silvieri was another of the neighborhood kids that Kevin grew up with. Dom had been into gambling as far back as Kevin could remember. His uncle was a numbers guy from Arthur Avenue. Dom was doing football sheets as far back as eighth grade. He jumped into the family business right before high school graduation. He was lucky he made it – the Dean of Students at St. Raymond's never liked Dom, and when he was caught taking bets on the basketball game against Cardinal Spellman High School, it took weeks of detention to placate him. It didn't help that Dom had Spellman picked by ten points.

"Yeah, good idea. I would've heard anyway. That's a lot of money. What else did she say?"

"She said he went to work Thursday morning, and she was expecting him home just like any other day, but he didn't pop up until after midnight. He never called, and then he wouldn't tell her anything when he showed up, he just lay in the bed staring up at the ceiling. The next morning, he split before she woke up."

"It sounds like a dope binge, but I never had Anthony figured that way."

"Nah. That crossed my mind too, but that's not him either. I spoke to him a couple weeks ago, and he was fine. It's not a drug thing."

"I'm sorry, Kevin. I'm at a loss. I haven't heard anything that would make any sense out of this. I haven't seen Anthony in a long time. The last time was when the both of you were in here together, and that was better than two years ago." Jimmy's eyes went soft and he reached across the booth and curled his hand around the back of Kevin's neck. "You see what happens when you guys forget about Jimmy. If you would just stop in once in a while and keep in touch, we could all keep an eye out for each other."

"It ain't easy, Jimmy. We're not kids anymore. I'm working fifty or sixty hours a week to try and save a couple of bucks to get a house. We've been in that damn apartment too long. I think that's what's getting to Ann Marie."

"What's that all about?"

"I don't want to talk about that now. I've got to figure out this Anthony thing first."

The door to the Emerald Bar opened and closed, pushing a shot of cool air into the room. Jimmy looked over at the bar. No one had gotten up to leave, someone must have come in. He stood up from the seat and scanned the room.

"Well, put away your thinking cap. Your answers just walked in the door," Jimmy said, motioning for Kevin to look behind him.

Kevin twisted in the booth and looked back into the room. There was Anthony slipping onto a stool at the end of the bar. Kevin stood and was about to head for Anthony, but Jimmy stopped him.

"Why don't you stay here, have some privacy. You need me to stick around?"

"No, Jimmy. Let me talk to him."

"Okay. I'll send him over," Jimmy said. "But before you go, come see me."

Kevin watched as Jimmy went back behind the bar, tied the white apron around his thick middle and worked his way down the bar to Anthony. Anthony barely reached up to shake Jimmy's hand. Jimmy pointed over at the table where Kevin was waiting. Anthony gave it a sidelong glance, then slowly walked over to the booth. He slid onto the seat across from Kevin wordlessly.

"Hey, man. What's going on? How the hell did you end up here?" Kevin asked.

Anthony looked terrible. His clothes were tired and hung from his body in desperation; his hair was rubbed flat - even as Kevin watched him, one of Anthony's hands mindlessly combed across his head. His eyes were bloodshot and blinked rapidly like window shades that kept rolling up after being yanked down.

Anthony didn't speak right away, he just looked out across the room. It was obvious to Kevin that Anthony was seeing something different than everybody else in the Emerald that night. There was definitely something behind Anthony's eyes that was affecting what was in front of them.

This is not a drug thing. This guy's just losing it.

Kevin's sense of alarm began to slip into controlled panic. His friend was somewhere now that Kevin didn't know how to get to. Anthony was on the edge of something Kevin couldn't measure.

I'll just wait him out. Let him tell me what's going on when he's ready. I mean, he's got to know something's going on. Just seeing me here like this has got to make him think.

Anthony smiled a sickly smile as he looked out across the room of the Emerald.

"Somebody raided the place. Who are all these people? They raided the fucking place," he said flatly. "They just move right in and push everything else out the fucking door."

"What are you talking about, man? Who?"

"These people, Kevin. Don't you see it, don't you feel it? This isn't our place anymore. There's nothing left. Jimmy fucking sold us out."

"Anthony, what are you talking about?" Shit! This guy's gonna' lose it here. "Jimmy didn't do anything, Anthony. What's this all about?""

"Come on, Kevin. Look around."

He still didn't look at Kevin; he kept staring out across the dimly lit room as if he was trying to not only look through the people, but across time.

"This was our place, man. You know how much time we spent here! We left pieces of our lives in here, man; and we trusted Jimmy with all of that. We trusted him like a banker, but look, he just gave everything away. We come back for them little pieces and there's nothing here. We've been replaced with these people. We helped make this place, and we come back and get shuffled off to "the booth". Jimmy's little lecture booth. Whenever he wanted to get on our case, we got sent to the booth for a fucking lecture. I don't need any lectures, Kevin. They're always a little late."

"We didn't come back, Anthony. And I didn't come here looking for any piece of myself, I came here looking for you."

"Looking for me?" Anthony finally turned and looked at Kevin. His eyes sought Kevin's with a rage. "You don't need to come looking for me. I don't need you to look for me, Kevin. I...oh, wait a minute. Now I see. You're right, we didn't come here. You were already here, in "the booth". You weren't looking for me. You were waiting for me. You're gonna' lecture me too, Jimmy Junior? The big man can't even do it himself anymore, so he recruited you. He made sure he sent me right over when I walked in the door. You know what, Kevin? Fuck you, and fuck your friend Jimmy. You guys want to be the big men? Well, where were you guys when I needed you? Fuck you both, Kevin."

Anthony stood to leave when Kevin spoke.

"Where are you going now, Anthony?"

"Fuck you, Kevin."

Kevin had reached the end of his rope of patience. He had endured too many "fuck you"s for one night. He wasn't about to chase Anthony all over the Bronx tonight, but he owed some kind of answer to Christine, and Ann Marie.

"Hey, asshole," he called out as Anthony left the table. "What do you want me to tell your wife?"

Anthony stopped in his tracks. He didn't turn, but his angry body seemed to deflate as he stood there in the dim light of the bar room. Kevin spoke again.

"Do you think it was my idea to just come and sit here out of the blue in the chance that one of my friends might just walk through the door?"

Anthony turned back toward Kevin. Mr. Hyde had stormed from the booth, but Dr. Jekyll returned and slid back onto the bench. He was silent for a moment, but then started slowly. A bittersweet smile replaced the sickly one that he wore a moment ago.

"This was our place, Kev. You do remember that, right?"

"Yeah, man. I remember it." Kevin sensed the return of his old friend and was ready to listen to whatever was tearing him up.

"Do you remember the time we all went over to that night game at Spellman High School? There was you and me and Joey and Tiv, remember that?"

"Yeah, sure, but we can't just sit here and bullshit about old times, Anthony. You gotta' tell me what's going on. You disappeared, and then you turn up here. What the hell is going on?"

Anthony just continued as if Kevin hadn't even spoken.

"It was just about this time of year, but it was a really nice night, kinda' warm. We never went to games over there, but Joey knew that kid on Spellman's team. I think he was a defensive back...no, no, he was a receiver."

Kevin just let him roll with it. *I hope this is going somewhere.*

"Then after the game, when we were leaving, Joey started in with those kids from the other school? There was the kid screaming that Spellman sucked, and Joey threw the can at him."

Kevin's mind was too far into the events of the night to allow himself any past returns.

"I don't know, Anthony. We did so much stuff back then."

"Joey ended up with a huge fat lip, he was bleeding all over the place, but he didn't want stitches. We were gonna' drag him to Jacobi Hospital, but he ran back here."

"Anthony, Joey had a fight just about every day since I met him in Third grade. I even gave him a black eye once or twice myself. He was a big mouth who never knew when enough was enough. I couldn't even begin to count every night he got us into some kinda' shit."

"But you'd remember this one, Kevin. We came back here and Jimmy iced him up and he slept here that night because he didn't want his father to see his lip."

The image of a beaten up Joey Patone renewed itself in Kevin's mind, but like he told Anthony - that was the only image he had of Joey. Joey started fights everywhere he went, and he usually lost. Kevin wondered if he would even recognize Joey after all these years without split lips or shiners. He saw that Anthony needed him to recall that night and the only thing that would stop him was if Kevin agreed.

"Yeah, Anthony. I think so."

"Yeah, you do," said Anthony, finally satisfied, and grateful.

Once Kevin seemed to acknowledge Anthony's urgency, he fell back into the booth and stared out across the room again, scanning time with pained eyes. After a few silent moments, he began again.

"I saw him," Anthony said from somewhere across the distance of where he was and where Kevin was.

"Saw who? Joey?"

"No, Kev. I saw the kid." Anthony's voice was flat and lifeless.

"What kid?"

"The kid from that night."

"You're losing me, Anthony. What kid?"

"You remember…"

Kevin had had enough of being lost in Anthony's thoughts. I can't take this anymore.

"No, Anthony. I don't remember. You've got to stop this memory lane shit. You're someplace else and I don't have a fucking clue what you're talking about."

Kevin reached across the table and took his friend's closed fist into his own. He pulled Anthony from his sunken place in the dark booth and slid his other hand behind Anthony's neck, pulling his face close to his.

"I'm a little worried here, Anthony. You're falling apart and I don't know what to do for you. You've been my friend for my whole life and all of a sudden it's like none of that counts for shit. Just tell me what the hell is going on. Christine told me about the money. Is somebody leaning on you? I'll go with you wherever you have to go, we'll take care of it tonight, just tell me what you need."

"I saw the kid, Kevin. The kid from that night." Anthony just continued, as if he had no choice but to tell the story. "After Joey started on one of those kids, another one ran up from behind and cold-cocked Joey. He went down like fucking Leon Spinks. You had already left, I think. Ann Marie was waiting for you or something, and you left before it all started. I saw you later, after we came back here." His tone was nearly begging for Kevin to summon up the same memories. "Anyway, Joey got cracked by this other kid who must have been a friend of the kid Joey was pounding on, and me and Tiv ran up on him and Tiv dropped him with an elbow to the back of his head. His friend ran off when he saw us take him down. Joey jumped up and started kicking this other kid as he lay on the ground. Me and Tiv joined in. This kid had curled up in a ball…like a baby, you know."

Anthony's eyes went back looking for this place in time as he spoke. Kevin could see the pain twisting his friend's face as he wracked his mind.

"It was so fucked up, Kevin. The three of us kicking this baby on the ground."

Anthony's eyes welled as if they wanted to cry, but something behind them cruelly denied them their release.

"Somebody yelled something at us, and Joey and Tiv took off, but just before I left, I cut loose one last kick into this kid. I think it was the hardest kick I ever gave anything, Kevin." His voice stumbled as if in disbelief of his own words. "I kicked him right between the shoulders, and I heard it…I heard the fucking crunch. I could feel it in my leg as I connected with him. I could feel the cracking,

Kevin. I knew I hurt this kid and I ran the fuck outta' there and never told anybody about it. We were all just kids. When you're sixteen and seventeen, you're like fucking invincible, you know. You're supposed to do this kind of shit, but you never figure somebody to get hurt for real."

His last sentence was more of a plea than a statement. Anthony needed to convince himself that it was possible, that youth made you like Superman. That when you got knocked down, you just picked yourself up and dusted yourself off. You lived to fight another day.

"Anthony, we all had fights back then. It was part of growing up. You can't look back now and ..."

"No, Kevin."

"...start blaming yourself. You even said this kid jumped on Joey. So he took a beating, he probably..."

"NO, KEVIN!"

Anthony's voice stopped Kevin in his words. His eyes were bulging and wide, rolling on the verge of exploding and spreading their horrible vision all over the walls of the Emerald Bar.

"No, Kevin. Listen to me, please. I saw this kid. I saw him on Thursday. I saw him, Kevin." He didn't want Kevin to try and reason it away, but to let him finish, to let him confess. Anthony continued slowly. "I saw him on Thursday. I went to check out a job over near Co-op City. It's like a convalescent place, like a long-term facility only not for seniors, more for people who can't take care of themselves, people with head injuries and in wheelchairs and stuff. It was a straight up bid – a new bathroom with a big walk in shower. After about a half-hour, I was done with the estimate - easy job, I'm thinking - then I call for the director to let him know I'm done. He asks me to come to his office. 'It's just down the hall on the right,' he says, 'past the Physical Therapy room.' So I gather up my stuff and head down the hall. I walk past the big doors of the Physical Therapy room - they're double-wide doors, you know, for the wheel chairs and beds - and I stopped to look in. It's a nice clean place, all white tile and bright lights. Not bad, I thought. These people got it okay here."

Anthony's face was featureless now. His mouth was just a thick line drawn across the hanging skin of his face. All of the effort of his anguish was measured in his eyes. They were there in the Physical Therapy room with his tormented mind.

"I stopped to look in, Kevin. It's that sick thing where you always want to look at these poor fucking bastards and then kiss God's feet that you're not one of them. I guess I wanted that feeling, that comfort, to know that I can just look at them there strapped to beds, stuck in wheelchairs, and feel sorry for them and glad for myself at the same time and then just carry on my merry way. It didn't work this time, though. God pulled a fast one on me. No feet to kiss anymore, no more merry way."

Anthony's body twisted in the booth as if in guilty reminder that he wasn't one of those "poor bastards". He could move, he could just walk on by and not even give it a second thought and it was as if his body bore the guilt.

"Then I saw him, Kevin. He was there in a wheel chair with straps across his chest holding him up, his arms and legs just wasted away and hanging off of him. He's like a scarecrow, just a head stuck on a bunch of broken old sticks. That's all he is now because of me - a fucking scarecrow."

"Anthony, how can you be sure that this is the same kid?" Kevin had sat in captive disbelief as Anthony told his story.

I can't believe this. This was years ago; this can't be the same kid.

"You're talking about something that happened more than ten years ago. You even said it happened so fast. How can you remember somebody that you saw once for less than a minute all those years ago?" Kevin not only needed this to be a mistake for Anthony's sake, but for his own as well. This couldn't be happening to his friend, to one of them.

"Kevin, it might have been ten years ago for us, but it was ten seconds ago for this kid. Time ended for him when I kicked him in the back. In a way, I guess, it ended for me too. I knew that something wasn't going to be right about this whole thing. I knew right then and there. When I cut loose on that kid, his head snapped back and his face burned itself into my brain. I knew I went over the edge. I might have pushed it back in my head, but I knew it was there. I ran away from that football field, but no matter how hard or fast I did, it didn't matter because it was already inside me. He had crawled inside me. The minute I saw him, I knew. It was ten seconds ago for me too, right there in that doorway."

The two sat in silence for a minute. Kevin had shrunk back into the booth, his mind barely able to get a grip on all that his friend had just told him.

This isn't right. Shit like this isn't supposed to happen. How the fuck can this be real? And not Anthony. Not him. This guy has got the charmed life. It's not fair to just take all that away. No, this isn't...

"Darren Freeman."

Anthony's voice sliced across Kevin's thoughts.

"What?" Kevin said, still split between his own thoughts and Anthony's words.

"Darren Freeman. That's his name." Anthony's twitching body fell still and his voice went grave and was devoid of the guilty ramblings that had given over his tale so far. It was as if he just wanted to get the rest out, to purge his head as wholly as possible.

Kevin didn't have any response to this. I don't want to know his name, he thought. *I don't want him to be real.*

"I asked the orderly when I slipped back into the hall. He didn't see me, Darren, I don't think. I asked the orderly how he got like that and he said he couldn't tell me, it was 'patient privilege'. He said I could ask him myself, but there was no way I could face him like that. I can't stare down into that scarecrow in the chair that I put him in and ask him how he got there." A tiny piece of whatever humanity Anthony still allowed himself lined across his brow. "It's something, how you've got all the balls in the world when you're a kid, but then when you get older, they're gone. Somehow, they just disappear."

A sudden thought bounded back into Kevin's head. *The money.* The eighty-five thousand dollars that Christine said was missing.

"What about the money, Anthony? What was with all that money?"

"I gave it to Darren Freeman this morning. After I saw him on Thursday, I was fucking lost. It all came back so fast, I had to do something. Friday morning, I went down to the bank and asked to withdraw everything. They told me I couldn't just take all that money, that Christine would have to sign for it too because her name's on the account with mine. They gave me some forms and I took them and forged Christine's signature on them and brought them back this morning. I got a bank check and brought it over to the rehab place and told the director that it was for Darren. For whatever he needed. I had to, Kevin. I have to. I have to give him everything because I took everything away from him. Everything I've got is built on a fucking lie. A lie that I told myself, and dragged Christine into."

"Is that the answer, Anthony? Just give him your whole life?" Kevin became angry. Angry at his friend for fucking up his life, the life that Kevin had always looked up to. He was angry that his friend may be mortal just like Kevin, even more so. He was angry that his friend had been tagged by fate to lose, when Kevin counted on him to always be the winner. If Anthony was a loser then what did that make him?

He was angry with Darren Freeman for being on that football field all those years ago, for being stupid enough to stand up instead of running. *You stupid, stupid fuck. Look what it got you! Where's that friend now? He ran as soon as you started getting your ass kicked in. You protected a fucking coward and it cost you everything. He ran, and my friend has to go down. You deserve that fucking rolling prison, that scarecrow body. You deserve to be alone inside your head, alone with your stupid mind, to relive that night over and over.*

"Is that it, Anthony? You're going to trade your life for his." Kevin was nearly in tears, he could feel them burning away at his eyes. "You're going to make up for this? You can't. You can't because it's not just you and this kid on some football field anymore; it's you and Christine. It's you and me and everybody else who cares about you, who need you to stay here and not go back to some place in the past. It's done, man. IT'S FUCKING DONE! IT'S OVER!"

Kevin's anger surprised him. He could feel the pure rage burning in his body. *NO! No way is this going to be how Anthony's life turns out. Maybe me, or Joey, or somebody else, but not Anthony. Not him.*

"Not you," he said softly, his anger dripping from his eyes in warm teardrops. "Not you, Anthony. Please. Let it go. You can't make it better by destroying yourself. You can't switch places with him. This is just the way life has played itself out. Let me just take you home. You gave him the money, that'll help him somehow. Come on, Anthony. Please, man. Let it go."

Anthony sat across from Kevin with his head hanging heavy from his neck. His shoulders had slumped and he had sunk so far into the booth that he looked half the size that he was. *My God. This must be what this kid looks like. Anthony is turning into him right before my eyes.*

Anthony spoke softly, but firmly to Kevin.

"I'm sorry, Kev. I can't let it go. I can't go past it because I've never gotten past it. I've been waiting for this. I knew it was coming. I knew I was on borrowed time, that I was just one step ahead of it. I snatched up the life I had all these years because I knew it was coming, and now the time is here. It's time to pay up. It's funny how I've been running all this time from a guy who can't even walk, and he caught me." An empty laugh escaped him as he said this. It wasn't the irony of his statement that prompted it; it was more the way fate had fucked him. His own success had led him right back to his greatest failure.

"I've got to face him, Kevin. I've got to do it and I'm scared shit. I wasn't scared of this guy when he was standing on two legs, I didn't give a second thought to jumping right on him then. But, I'm scared of him now. I'm scared of a fucking head on a stick. I'm so scared of him, scared that I might never be able to walk up to him and say 'I'm sorry'."

Anthony looked into his friend's eyes. Kevin saw the fear that overshadows the fear of pain or even death. Kevin saw in Anthony's eyes the fear of living without forgiveness.

"I can't let it go. It has to be him, he's got to do it, but he might never let it go, Kevin. He's holding me in his lifeless curled up hands and he might never let me go. That's what I'm scared of. What if I do it and he never lets me go? What if I say 'I'm sorry' and he just sucks me into his dead world? I'll be trapped with him in that lifeless body forever. I would rather trade places with him than be there with him. I'm so fucking scared, Kevin."

Kevin felt his guts crash inside his body. So much of the present was woven together with his past, and now it was all coming apart before him, and his friend, one of the biggest elements of his life, was the one unraveling it. His mind had nowhere to go with what was happening to Anthony, and him. The vision of Anthony trading places with the guy in the wheelchair played out in his head. He could see the scarecrow lifting himself from the cruel chair and Anthony taking his place, twisting and shrinking until he was no more than a head and a pile of sticks. It terrified Kevin. No nightmare that could ever erupt from inside of his mind could match the sheer horror of the one coming from outside it.

He had no words of comfort for his friend, and Anthony wouldn't accept any if he had. While Kevin had treasured his past for all these years, Anthony had been hiding from it. What Kevin had held dear, Anthony had dreaded. The idea of this made Kevin desperate in way that few people ever know. *This can't be real. It can't be fair. How can something just come along and deconstruct my life, defy my memories? All those times that I thought were the greatest times of our lives are lies? The guy that I thought was fearless, that I counted on, was running away from something all this time? If his life is a lie, then what is mine? What's real? What the fuck is real anymore?*

In that moment, Kevin saw himself in the barest way he ever had. He was weak, unable to relieve any of his friend's pain. Oh, he was a tough guy; he was going to come to his friend's rescue. He was ready to face a shylock's strong-arm, to wrestle a coke demon; he was ready to take on anything that was coming at his friend. I'll take care of this and be home in time for the second half of the game. Friendship overcomes fear, he had told himself. Just like the old days. But here he was, unable to handle what was coming from inside his friend. Kevin could give Anthony sympathy, but not empathy. He could give him pity, but not the forgiveness that he so dearly needed. Kevin was powerless against the ghost that had finally caught up with Anthony. He lost the battle for his friend's soul to a long past mistake. Kevin needed for this nightmare to end.

"Anthony, why don't you let me take you home? Christine is worried and probably pretty scared. You're going to have to tell her what's going on."

Anthony didn't respond right away, he just looked up at Kevin. His eyes were still wide, but they were clearer than before.

"No, Kevin. I'll go home on my own. I can't put you in the middle of this."

"I'm already in it, Anthony."

Anthony looked over at Kevin and at the moment Kevin knew that there was nothing that he could do for him. This was something that only Anthony could handle. All the years that had passed before Anthony's eyes had been wiped away. They were stuck somewhere that Kevin couldn't get to, that Kevin could never know, but for a fleeting second, they reached down into Kevin and released him from those bonds of friendship that would only drag him down with him. I'm alone, his eyes told Kevin.

"No, Kev. You go home. I know what you're trying to do, but I've got to do this on my own. It's not your thing." He paused as he looked at his friend. "Thanks, Kevin."

Kevin could only nod. His heart seemed to pound in his throat.

"You were smart enough to go back to Ann Marie that night, be smart again," Anthony said. As Kevin sat in the ruins of the lives of two friends, one thought began to push its way through - Ann Marie.

Ann Marie. If it wasn't for her, I would have been there to stop Anthony, or maybe it wouldn't have happened at all. If it wasn't for her, it might have... been me.

She was as big a part of his past as Anthony - even more, she was his future. Ann Marie was always there when his life was good, and when it was bad. She was the one waiting for him even after he had left her behind. She was right. She was always there when he came back. He suddenly realized just how much he had taken for granted back then, and now. He was wishing he would've listened to her tonight and stayed behind with her. It was safe back in their little apartment; there were no terrible ghosts from the past snatching up memories and erasing lives. There was nothing to run from there. Anthony came to the Emerald tonight looking for some safeguarded pieces of his youth to reassure himself that he was once innocent. Kevin walked away from the very thing his friend sought. Kevin's innocence, his youth, his past, present, and future, were all being kept alive by Ann Marie. He was the cripple too, but he had salvation – Ann Marie. She could always make him whole whenever he reduced himself to pieces.

"Go ahead, man. I'll be okay." Anthony's voice betrayed itself.

No you won't, Kevin thought. Neither will I.

Kevin surrendered and cast one last glance into Anthony's eyes. That's it then. I let you down and I get to crawl away. I'm so sorry, Anthony. Sorry I couldn't make this go away. I'm, sorry I wasn't more of a friend. Anthony nodded to Kevin as if he could read his thoughts.

Kevin rose from the booth slowly and began to walk away. He turned back to Anthony and said, "Call me soon, okay? Just let me know that you're okay." Anthony didn't respond, he was still and silent. He's already gone, Kevin thought.

Kevin walked up to the bar; Jimmy was already waiting for him there at the end.

Jimmy could tell from Kevin's face that things hadn't gone well.

"Everything okay, Kevin?" It was one of those questions that come out already answered.

"No, Jimmy. Everything's not okay, but there's nothing I can do about it." Kevin's eyes moved toward the booth, but his head couldn't muster the courage to turn with them. "He'll be leaving soon, I think. Just let him be."

"Sure, Kevin. How about you, you okay?"

Kevin thought about Jimmy's question. No, I'm not okay. I let my friend down. It was my shot to be more than a mouthful of promises, but that's pretty much all I am.

"I'll survive."

"You gonna' stay for a little of the game," Jimmy asked. Kevin glanced up at the television. Dennis Miller was making some banal comment about Miami's quarterback.

"Nah. Ann Marie's waiting. I hope."

"I wanted to ask you about that. Everything alright with you two?"

He thought about the earlier events of the night, of walking out on her again. "I don't know."

"Maybe she's just waiting for something from you?"

"From me?" Kevin had reached his limit for letting people down. "You know what, Jimmy? This is just not my fucking night. I'll see you around."

"Wait, Kevin, wait. I'm not breaking your balls for no reason. Let me just tell you something before you go storming into the night. Back when you and Ann Marie were first getting together, I would watch you do so many stupid things that should have left you pulling your pud like a loser instead of lucking out with a girl like her. This girl was nuts about you, and you used to do everything in your power to screw that up. Do you know how many times she sat crying in this bar, crying after you?"

Kevin listened with his head down.

"Do you know how many times you took off with your boys and left her at the curb like a dog?"

What - has everybody been watching me my whole life? Does everybody know what a fucking asshole I am? Kevin couldn't handle much more. Maybe it would be easier to run like Anthony had been doing his whole life. Kevin had no scarecrows in his closet, only himself.

"You know what, Jimmy? I've heard this already tonight. I'm such a bad guy. I'm trying to help my fucking friend, and all I'm getting is what a bad guy I am. Maybe Anthony saw the fucking light before I did? Maybe just taking off is not such a bad thing?"

"Kevin," Jimmy's voice was soft, but firm. Kevin stopped and looked at him. There was something about the big man that let him pull off all this big brother shit. "Just hang on. No one is saying that you're a bad guy. You're just the opposite, kid. That's what this is all about. It's never easy being a good guy. The shit always comes down on you, but that's why people count on you. I'm sure it wasn't easy for Anthony's wife to call you with this, but she did. If Ann Marie is pissed, it's because she knows that. She's probably still afraid of losing you. All those tears back when she was a kid were about losing you. They just get a little bit harder to swallow when you get older. One time, after you had taken off on her yet again, I made a deal with Ann Marie to give you a second chance. I told her that if you came in here one day, ready to throw in the towel on yourself, that I would find a way to let her know that you made the right choice. Well, it's the moment of truth, Kevin. We all hit a point in our lives where we doubt ourselves, where we wonder if we're still the same people we thought we were, or thought we would be. Well, you are, Kevin. You're still a good guy. You wouldn't have come here tonight if you weren't"

Kevin was quiet now. *Damn Jimmy. This guy always has to make sense. Why can't I find a bartender who'll just pump me full of watered down beer, scam me for tips, and push me out the door. No, I gotta' find the one with the fucking heart.*

"You still love her?"

Kevin hesitated a second, not because he didn't know the answer, but because he wanted to measure his words. *I put my foot in my mouth so many times tonight, it's a wonder I have any teeth left.*

"Yeah, Jimmy. More than I guess I know."

"That's what I figured." Jimmy grabbed him around the back of neck again. For somebody who spent all of his nights handling cold beer, his big hands were warm. "Let her know you came to see me tonight. Tell her I said 'hello'. Just don't leave her at the curb anymore, Kevin. Okay?"

Kevin looked up at Jimmy, and nodded. He knew that Jimmy was right. Things had gotten a little too busy, too easy to take things out on each other.

Jimmy the Talking Torso strikes again.

"Alright, Jimmy. I gotta' go."

"Next time you decide to drop in, bring her along. I'd like to see her," said Jimmy.

"If she's still there when I get back."

"She always was."

Just before Kevin left the Emerald, he glanced up into the big glass window of the bar. He could see Anthony reflected in its dark glass, slumped there in the booth. *He's gone. He's the scarecrow now.* Kevin could see right through the reflection of his friend into the night outside. It was like looking through a ghost. He thought about all the ghosts of the Emerald, the "little pieces" of themselves that Anthony talked about, haunting the place. He looked through his own reflection and into the night. *I gotta' get out of here before I leave* everything *behind.*

For the second time that night, Kevin walked through the door of the little apartment. There was no fluttering phone to greet him this time, only silence. As he hung his jacket on its empty hook, he listened through the quiet for any sign of Ann Marie. The only sounds in the apartment were the ones he made as he dropped his shoes by the closet door. As he walked out of the hallway, his foot connected with something heavy. His big toe throbbed with pain and the ashtray went sliding across the floor. *I knew that thing would get me somehow. I've got to throw that damn thing out.* He hobbled into the kitchen. It was dark and quiet. The little red and chrome chair that Ann Marie had been sitting on was still there; pulled away from the table like it was when he left, only this time it was empty. *This doesn't look good. I hope she's still here.*

He walked into the living room. The lights were off, as was the television. She liked to watch the news, but the glass tube was dark and silent. No news is good news, he laughed nervously to him self. Then he saw her. Ann Marie was curled up in a corner of the couch. She was tiny again, no more angry giant, no more 800lb. gorilla. Just his wife. He watched her as she slept there. *Still here. Always here.*

"Jimmy was right." He spoke softly to her as she lay there sleeping. "What he told you once. He was right. You were right. I'm sorry, baby. I'm sorry for everything. I hope you can forgive me."

He sat down on the couch next to her and looked over at her again, only now her eyes were open. He could see them glistening in the dim light. *Was tonight the last straw? Had I left her behind one too many times?*

She slid across the couch and put his face in her hands. She looked into his eyes and saw that the night had somehow changed him. She sensed that she would never be left behind again. She let go of his face, dropped her head into his lap, and curled up against his body. He let his hand fall to her soft face and he brushed her hair away.

Thank you, Jimmy.

Her soft voice broke the silence. "Did you find Anthony?"

I don't know. I found somebody, but not Anthony, at least not the Anthony I went looking for.

His silence answered for him.

"You missed a good game tonight," she said, letting him off the hook for now. "The Jets won for a change."

"Oh, was there a game on tonight," he feigned.

Ann Marie laughed. "You're an asshole."

He was never so happy to hear those words.

PRIMA

He poked the half-sleeping woman lying next to him on the messy bed. She made no move to acknowledge him, so he poked her again a little harder.

"Hey, guess what I heard last night?"

Sunlight was mercilessly filling the room through the unshielded wide windows; she could hear Christina already mulling about in the kitchen - probably dumping the whole box of Cap'n Crunch all over the floor – and Paul was playing guessing games. It was not how she imagined her Saturday morning when her head hit the pillow last night, the hours seeming like mere minutes to her weary body. Sheets were pulled haphazardly over her head; one leg, exposed to the knee, was hanging off the edge of the bed. Her head was throbbing slightly from what she could only imagine were allergies – no such luck in it being a hangover. Paul was the one out at the Emerald last night. She had been the one up past midnight consoling her sister Gina over another fight with Nick. It was Gina's hysterical phone call and tear-drenched arrival that sent Paul fleeing to Jimmy B.'s bar stools in the first place, much to his obvious elation. Gina's final departure at one a.m. and Paul's subsequent return at nearly two didn't leave much of a window for mental reconstruction. He came home with Budweiser babble, packing wood - neither of which she was in the mood for. Her hope was that he would sleep both off, yet here he was poking her, though thankfully with his finger this time. Where was the fucking justice in this world?

"Hey, guess what I heard last night?" he said again.

"You poke me one more time and I swear that finger will be the only thing sticking straight out of you for a month," she growled from under her sheet-covered head.

"Come on, Tina," wake up. "I ran into Jerry the Dutchman at Jimmy B.'s. You gotta' hear this."

"For Christ's sake Paul, I'm really tired. Your daughter is making a mess in the kitchen. Go take care of her."

"Christina!" he called out loudly, making her ears rattle. "Don't make a mess. Mommy will make your breakfast in a minute."

Why do I bother? she thought.

"Come on, Tee. Turn over for a second," he said.

"No. The Dutchman is an asshole. He was always an asshole. I couldn't care less what he had to say when we were teenagers, and I care even less now."

Paul leaned in and pressed himself across Tina's back. She groaned an audible "ugh!" from his weight upon her.

"You're crushing me you fucking oaf!" she forced out with her escaping breath, and kicked her legs backward striking Paul in the thigh.

He backed off and rubbed away an emerging Charlie Horse. "That's fucked up, Tee. I had to flee my own home because of Gina, who chewed your ear off for hours, and then all I get is your face buried in the pillow."

She reached up and pulled the sheets from her head. "Oh, it's okay when my head is buried in the pillow for other reasons though, huh? And don't use my sister as an excuse. You didn't have to *flee* anywhere. You look for any ploy to go see your friends -that bunch of losers. You guys are all thirty or better, yet you still act like fucking high-schoolers. If I hadn't dragged your ass into the real world, you would still be a juvenile yourself."

She slammed her face back into the pillow and pulled the sheets back over her head.

"That's nasty, Tee. These people were your friends once too."

These people were never my *friends*, she mentally murmured. *They were walking hard-ons looking to* fuck *all my friends. You should only know how many of* your *friends tried to get into my pants when your back was turned. We'd see who you'd defend then, Paul.*

He waited a few seconds and poked Tina again. Hard kicks came flying at him from under the sheets. He peeled the sheets back again.

"Come on, I don't like talking to the back of your head."

She realized she would never get rid of him until she let him spill his little nugget of barroom bullshit.

"WHAT already!" she screamed from her pillow, twisting to look her pain-in-the-ass husband in the eyes. "WHAT!"

She could see that Paul had something that he found interesting to tell her. She felt bad for giving him a hard time, but she was truly drained, both physically and mentally.

"Come on, Paul. What is so damn important?"

He hesitated and grinned like the Cheshire cat. "Guess who's coming back?"

She plopped her face back down into the pillow. "I'm not playing guessing games. When you're done busting the balls I don't have, tell me your little story."

"Okay, okay," he continued. "Frankie Calabro."

Tina sank hard into the bed as if Paul had sat on her back again, but she knew that he hadn't. It was his words that pressed down on her this time. *Frankie Calabro.*

Her breath stuck in her lungs for an eternity and she couldn't urge any words from her mouth. *Oh my God! Frankie Calabro is coming back? How can that be?*

"How can that be?" The words surprisingly escaped

her strangled throat. "I thought he was in Chicago or someplace?"

"He was," Paul said, knowing he had piqued Tina's interest, but not for the simple reason of gossip that he assumed. There was something more to her curiosity that she held back from him.

Tina deliberately kept her face in her pillow. She wanted to keep her display of apathy alive, and she knew her face would give away her distress at this turn of events. She mustered as much of a renewed pugnacity as she could and engaged her charade.

"Why would he come back? It's probably a rumor, Paul. You are all such little boys when you get together and drink. You gossip like old women."

"Nah, Tina. The source is good on this one," he said with an affirming nod.

"I already told you - Jerry is an asshole. You can't believe anything that shit-head says. He's named after a fucking cigar, Paul."

"No, no, Tee," Paul responded, taking her bait. "Not just a cigar. Jerry was a pioneer in the art of hollowing out a cheap stogie and stuffing it with reefer. He was years ahead of the *blunt*. The man is nearly a legend."

"Maybe a legend among you and your moron friends, but completely an asshole to the rest of the world."

"You're still pissed over him and Gina. Jerry was nearly family, Tee, or are you forgetting how many *'but I love him'* tears came pouring out of her over that fucked relationship too." Paul was treading the "how fucked up your sister is" waters and decided to dive deeper. "You know, I heard she was a bit of a cigar pioneer herself - a little pre-Lewinsky, if you catch my drift."

Though she hated when Paul picked on her sister, she was glad that the conversation was moving away from its heart. She would run with it. Anything to divert Paul from exploring the possibility that Frankie Calabro may show up in the neighborhood again.

"You are a pig, Paul. And that's what I'm talking about. Jerry made up all kind of stories about Gina and you bought them all. The guy is a fucking liar and a loser. His word means shit."

"Maybe so, but the word comes from a higher source – the Dutchman's mother!" Paul crossed his arms over his chest as if he had just laid an indisputable fact on the table.

"Mrs. Morano? So you're not only gossiping *like* an old woman, you are gossiping *with* an old woman."

"I didn't get it right from her. Like I said, Jerry told us. She's what you would call a 'credible witness', Tee."

"I wouldn't exactly call her credible, Paul."

"Just listen, Tee. You know how she's at like *every* mass over at St. Dominic's…

Probably praying for her asshole son, Jerry, a lot of good that'll do.

…well, Calabro's mother was there the other day and Mrs. Morano overheard her talking to the Monsignor about her son coming home."

Overheard? Right! Nothing gets past that nosy witch. She tormented Gina the entire time she was with Jerry the loser. Like her son was too good for my sister. It's unbelievable that a person can't even find peace or privacy in a church.

The prospect of the rumor being more bullshit than fact began to ease the weight on her chest.

Maybe Mrs. Calabro was just praying that Frankie would come home?

She leaned up from the pillow and confronted Paul. As long as she could keep the tone of the conversation contentious, she could mask her mounting anxiety.

"Oh, so it's second-hand hearsay now. Just like I said - bullshit. Now go and make something for your daughter to eat. You have to take her to soccer practice at nine o'clock." Tina turned and again buried her face in her pillow, effectively dismissing Paul. "I'm staying in bed."

"Wait, wait, wait," Paul said.

Shit. He can never just let things go.

"Forget about the Dutchman and his mother for a minute; what if it is true? What if Frankie Calabro is coming back? Do you realize what a fucking war is going to break out around here?"

Around here! What does he mean by that? Her chest crashed in on itself again, worse than before.

Paul's voice suddenly seemed to take on an ominous tone. "That prick followed no fucking rules. He didn't respect boundaries. No respect for other people's *property.*" The last word seemed to jump out of his mouth with a noticeable snap.

"Talk about a menace to society, there was a collective sigh of relief when that scumbag had to go on the lam. I'll tell ya', I for one was hoping that old man Perillo would have put the bullet in Calabro's head personally. I mean, shit, all that money that he stole - that he *beat* out of Dom Silvieri - was Perillo's vig and numbers cash. Dom still has a lisp from how bad his jaw was busted up by Calabro. Ten years is not enough time between him and this neighborhood. I wouldn't be surprised if he was dead less than a day after he gets back here. I don't think anybody would give a shit either way. Right, Tee? Do *you* think anybody would care?"

Tina's heart stopped beating. Dead. It was as if a hand had reached inside her chest and gripped the throbbing muscle like a piece of chop meat and crushed it, the pulpy mush squishing through its fingers. *Why* would *he be coming back now?*

The loud crash from the kitchen put an end to the conversation, and got Tina off the emotional hook, at least for now. She leapt from the bed and made for the door.

"Never mind, Paul. I'll take care of it. I'll take care of *everything,* as usual."

§

"Hello."

The voice was blunt and annoyed, as if the call was beyond a mere intrusion, more of an insult.

"Gina, it's me," Tina said, ignoring her sister's impertinence. It was typical morning-after-big-tearfest Gina attitude. Gina's form of depression was aggression. She was ready to eat her enemies, and anyone who called her when she was in this mood was an enemy.

"Why are you calling so early? I'm tired, Tee."

Early? It's almost noon. Tired! Like I wasn't there at one in the morning when you were crying your eyes out over that prick. You can be such a bitch. Tired...tough luck. It's my turn to dump on somebody.

"Did the asshole call you yet?" Tina figured she would disguise her own need to vent within Gina's festering love/hate for Nick. She gambled on "asshole" - sensing that he hadn't called to make-up yet. Gina's attitude would have been more *can't-talk-now-Nick's-here* if he had.

"No." Her flat response confirmed Tina's guess.

"Don't sit around all day waiting for him, Gina. Fuck him, if he doesn't call."

The silence on the other end of the phone kept the ball in Tina's court. She played it.

"Paul didn't come home until two. He was down at the Emerald with the rest of Jimmy Burke's Juveniles. He's out now with Christina at her soccer practice. I hope he has a hangover."

"He came home drunk? That's not right, Tina. He's a thirty year old man with a daughter. You need to watch him."

Tina sighed silently. Listening to Gina badmouth Paul was as bad as listening to him trash-talk about her. She was always in the middle. If any of this Calabro stuff was true, she would be in the middle again.

"Yeah, and he saw Jerry Morano down there." She knew that this was shaky ground. Gina would either feel that Tina was tallying up all her sister's romantic failures or she would jump on the bashing bandwagon. Either way, Tina needed to see if her sister had heard anything about Frankie

Calabro.

There was another brief eternity before Gina responded.

"He still hangs around at the Emerald? What a fucking loser. Thank God I shook him loose," came the response that let Tina finally exhale.

Shook him loose. You cried over him for weeks after you found out he was getting into Nancy O'Brien's pants, not that that took much. She felt her blood pressure rising over her sister's persistent state of denial. *Control it, Tina. Stay on track.*

"Jerry told Paul some story about Frankie Calabro coming home."

Tina paused to allow Gina to chime in with her typical "I know something you don't know" one–upping. Tina took the ensuing silence to mean that Gina hadn't heard anything about this yet. This was a good thing. One thing about Gina, she always had her ear to the ground. Tina had to agree with Paul's opinion of Gina as "one chatty bitch", even though she didn't like the way he put it. Gina was a veritable bulletin board of gossip and rumor in the neighborhood.

Tina was beginning to feel more relaxed. If Frankie Calabro hadn't registered on Gina's radar, the whole story had to be bullshit.

"Who knows if it's even true? Why would he come back anyway?"

More silence filled the telephone earpiece, only now it made Tina wary. The only thing more disconcerting than Gina yapping away is Gina with nothing to say.

"Holy shit, Tee. Why is *he* coming back?" Her voice was nearly a whisper, yet it carried that subtle tone of conspiracy and cover-up. Not a good sign, Tina thought.

"I don't know. I mean, besides his mother, I don't think he's got anybody left around here."

Gina's silence had suddenly become a third party to the conversation, and it spoke louder than either of them. Tina cut through it to find out what was going on in her sister's head.

"What, Gina?" Tina let some impatience slip out with her words, but there was clearly something that her sister was holding back. *Oh, no, Gina! Not him too! You weren't fucking around with this guy too!* "Gina, please tell me you and Frankie Calabro didn't…"

"Me, Tina? Me? I don't think we're talking about me anymore here."

It took a second for Gina's response to register. *Oh shit! What does she mean by that?*

Could Gina be fishing? She could never resist the urge to start a few rumors of her own, but she had never yet done it to her own sister. Did she suspect something, or worse, did she *know* something?

"What are you talking about, Gina?"

Their silent partner grabbed hold of the conversation again. *Well, what are you waiting for, Gina? Just fucking spill it!*

"Tina, I was there that night. The night Frankie split."

SHIT! Panic gripped her like a cop grabbing a kid by the collar. *Keep your head, Tina. Gina's almost always wrong about what she thinks she sees. She couldn't possibly know what happened.*

"Where, Gina? Where were you?" She tried to keep her voice light as if she was just playing her sister's game, but an unmistakable undertone of urgency belied her forced insouciance.

"Tina, I saw you. I saw you climbing out of Frankie's car the night before he left in a hurry."

"I saw you"? She saw *me in Frankie Calabro's car! Calm down, play it cool.*

"What? You saw *me*?"

"Don't lie to me. How do you think I felt watching my sister crawl out of the back of that dirt bag's car? I mean, everybody knew what a scumbag Frankie was, and here I am finding out the hard way that my *engaged* sister is…cheating on my boyfriend's friend with him."

"YOU STUPID BITCH!" The words jumped unguarded from her head to her lips! Even hearing her sister mention a passing notion about what happened with

Frankie Calabro was enough to stab her soul with a hot knife. Having Gina speculate about what she thinks she saw all those years ago was more dangerous than having her know the truth. For everyone.

Oh, shit, oh shit, oh, SHIT! This can't be real. If she said anything to anybody, even after all this time.

"WHAT! *BITCH!* Fuck you, Tina. All these years I came to you with everything and now when I want to be there for you, you call me a bitch! FUCK YOU, TINA!"

She ignored her sister's angry retort. She had endured so many of them through the years that they were reduced to mundane speed bumps in Gina's prattle. "Gina, what do you mean, 'you saw me? You have to tell me what you *think* you saw."

"Think, Tina? *Think!* I know what I saw, but bitches don't talk, Tina."

"GINA! I'm sorry, okay? I'm sorry. Now what did you see?"

Gina was in the catbird seat now. With an apology under one arm and her sister's secret under the other, she was Queen Shit.

"I was across the street with Jerry in a car. We were...talking about stuff." She left out that she was in the back seat of that car and the talking was restricted to her own instructions regarding the better positions for screwing in a car and Jerry's moans once he followed them.

Tina's mind raced back to that night. She was sure that no one saw her. The street was empty; she could still see it in her head. She made sure of it before she even walked down the block to Frankie's car. How could this be? In a car? There were some cars parked along the street but she didn't recognize any of them. Jerry Morano didn't even have a car; he was always borrowing someone else's. Then it hit her. Gina wasn't alone. She said she was there with Jerry.

"Jerry! Gina, are you telling me that Jerry Morano was there with you?"

Her silence confirmed Tina's assumption.

Holy shit. Jerry Morano. Jerry who started this whole Frankie Calabro story. Jerry the Dutchman who was with Paul last night. Can this get any worse? He must know. That's what this is all about.

Gina's voice was barely background noise to Tina now.

Those two idiots saw me, and that fucking asshole Jerry just had to open his mouth.

"I had to beg Jerry not to tell Paul. And just so you know, I was ready to dump him before this happened. I ended up staying with him all that extra time just to keep him quiet. So you should know how much I went through for you before you call me a 'bitch' again." Gina took a second to breathe. "I was kind of upset that you never came to me with this, but you always were the 'strong' one like Mommy and Grandma. I got more of Daddy's giving personality; you got sucked in by those fucking cold witches. But still, I'm your only sister, Tina. I mean she is my niece and god-daughter. I would do anything for her. Don't worry, Tina. If that bastard tries to touch Christina, I'll fucking stab him in the heart."

What? Wait a minute…what? Christina ? What does she have to do…Oh, my God! He doesn't know anything about her, unless word got back to him somehow.

"*Fucking* Frankie Calabro…is that what you think this is all about? And you think Christina…I can't believe you." Tina was talking as much to herself as she was to her sister. She had no air in her lungs and her heart flopped around in her chest like a fish on a boat dock.

"Tina, we both know that you wearing white on your wedding day was only for Daddy's sake. He may be old-fashioned enough to want to believe that Christina happened on your honeymoon, but I heard all the tears coming from your room every night before the wedding. And when you almost called it off, I was pretty sure it wasn't Paul you were crying over."

Tina looked over at the clock. It was well past noon. *Christina's soccer practice should have been over by now. Where the hell is Paul? Paul! What did Jerry tell Paul? Gina, what did your big mouth and your open legs do now?*

∫

Tina walked quickly, but with heavy steps. Her legs were throbbing from the double-step of her pace and she had already covered more ground than she knew, but even so, her legs were barely keeping up with her racing mind. She had gone over to the soccer fields and practice was already over. Paul and Christina were gone. Maybe he had taken her for lunch? She liked the pizza at Anthony's, but they weren't there. She didn't want to start calling around, raising any alarms just yet. She was trying to stay calm. She wasn't sure if sheer panic, damage control, or complete denial were her impetus now, but after her conversation with Gina, any or all of those options were driving her on. After a fruitless search in every place she could think of, only one place remained in the equation: Jimmy B.'s. – The Emerald Bar.

Though she had spent many of her teen years - and most of the waning afternoon - wearing out the soles of her shoes all over the weary concrete of the old Bronx neighborhood, she hadn't been on *this* street for years. She was here and she didn't want to be, but time and tide does indeed change everything.

Frankie Calabro was coming back.

As she neared the middle of the street she could feel more than see the face of the old bar. In spite of the full afternoon sun challenging any shadows on the sidewalk, an odd light joined it on the ground outside the bar, either a reflection off of the long glass window or an emanation from inside. Though there was no one outside the place now, she could see shades of the past coming and going, young men laughing and smoking, looking over the girls going in and out. All her friends were there, in eternal youth, hanging out the way only the young and the carefree could.

Even though the boys all laid claim to the memories made there, the girls of the neighborhood had some of their own. Just as much as the big talk and black eyes, big love and bruised hearts left their marks all over this place as well.

She brushed aside the ghosts and grabbed hold of the tarnished brass door handle.

In and out, Tina, she told herself. *There probably won't even be anybody in here at this time of day. I don't even know what made me think Paul would come here. His car is not even outside. He wouldn't come back here. Why would he? Alright, just slip in quietly, make sure he's not here and head right out. No one will even notice.*

She may as well have crashed through the big window because every head seemed to turn or glance or nod in the direction of her entrance.

Great! What did a desperate woman *alarm go off or something?*

There was no slipping in and out of Jimmy B.'s. Not as long as Jimmy Burke was behind the bar, and that was always. He could almost tell who walked in just by the way the door squeaked when it opened. His sixth sense prepared him for whatever game plan need be played and his play book was out.

Tina Mallick hadn't stepped foot in The Emerald Bar for years, yet Jimmy Burke knew her the second she walked through the door. The last time he had seen her, she was still Christina Gaetti. It was a week or so before her wedding to Paul Mallick - another old face Jimmy hadn't seen for years, until recently. A face that he knew was sitting at the back table of the Emerald Bar. As much as Jimmy loved seeing old faces back for a visit, having these two both in his bar at this time couldn't be a good thing.

He was already in Wife-Looking-For-Husband formation as Tina made her first steps into the bar, and in the world of men and bars, the bartender was the first line of defense. Avoiding a confrontation in the Emerald was always a priority, but protecting the quarterback was his natural instinct.

"Good things always come in pairs," he called out as she neared the bar. "First Paul stops in last night and now you. How are you, *Tina?*"

Jimmy Burke's voice seemed just a little too eager and a little too loud when he said her name. Tina sensed a deliberate distraction.

God damn it, Paul! You are here, you son of a bitch!

"I was just asking Paul last night about his beautiful bride who never comes back to say hello. If I remember, you were a big fan of Long Island Iced Teas. How about one for old times? On me, of course."

All of Tina's anxiety and anger came to a fine point in her head. She was in no mood for Jimmy and his glad-handing.

Asshole.

"This is no trip down memory lane, Jimmy. I'm looking for my husband." She didn't bother offering up a volley. "Where is he?"

Jimmy was trapped. As much as he had hoped to keep an obvious marital flare-up out of his bar, he had fumbled on the big play. He wouldn't lie, but he wouldn't allow her to tear through the Emerald like a woman scorned. Hell's fury would never trump Jimmy B.'s standing in his own bar. A bartender never recovered from a Judas kiss, and Jimmy wasn't about to go down.

As luck would have it, he wouldn't have to.

"Tina? What are you doing here?" came Paul's voice as he appeared from the back of the room. Her heart fluctuated between anger and fear with every beat. It stuck on fear the second she noticed Dominic Silvieri over Paul's shoulder. Dom, the one Frankie had beaten and robbed of Perillo's money all those years ago, years that have suddenly turned into yesterday. It's edgy and exciting to have a numbers runner as friend when you're both teens, but there is a tipping point when childhood friendships mean nothing compared to money and revenge. Paul and Dom weren't kids anymore.

What are you doing with him, Paul? What have you done? Where's my baby?

"Where's Christina, Paul?"

"Let's go outside," Paul said, sensing the eyes of Jimmy B. on him. He was clearly not in the same teasing, playful mood he was when he woke and poked her this morning. He clamped on her elbow and headed for the door. Tina straightened her arm and jerked it free of his grip. She found the door before Paul and didn't bother to hold it for him.

"Where's my daughter, Paul?" She rounded on him, words shooting from her mouth in jabs as they stepped out onto the sidewalk.

My daughter, she said. Her purposeful distinction did not miss its mark.

"*Our* daughter, Tina. We are talking about *our* daughter, right Tina?" Paul shot back. He paused for a moment to let the remark hang in the air. "She's with my mother," he finally said flatly.

Tina's chest nearly collapsed with relief as she exhaled the stale breath of panic that had been filling her lungs.

"You know what I meant, Paul. What where you thinking, taking her without telling me? I've been all over the fucking place looking for you! I'm a nervous wreck"

"I *took* her to soccer practice, like you told me to. Like I always do on Saturday. What would make you suddenly so nervous about that? You said you were tired from being up all night with your sister. I thought I was being thoughtful."

"Dumping her with your mother and sneaking off to the fucking bar is real thoughtful, Paul."

"My mother made us lunch and Christina fell asleep on the couch. I guess your sister kept her up all night too. Maybe your girl party was more of an initiation than a crisis? A little broomstick practice, maybe?"

Always blaming my family, Tina thought. She knew the broomstick reference was a shot at her grandmother, as well. Paul had always thought himself clever in referring to the women in her family as witches, with Nona as *Prima Strega,* head witch. In this case, it was welcome. Let him make it about Gina, about her grandmother, anybody but her. If it became about her, then it would become about Frankie. Then it would become about all of them.

"And so what if I came down here to see some of my old friends."

"Oh, so Dom is one of your buddies now? Were you two just talking about *old times*?" When Jimmy had offered her a drink for "old times" it had made her skin clench. It was as if he was taunting her. *Could he have overheard Jerry and Paul last night? Did he know something too?* Her chest filled with the freezing sting of panic that rushes in when your guard is down. *Did everybody know?*

"Yeah, Tee," he said slowly. His voice had become something more than sarcastic. It became…hateful. "Old times."

It was the bite of his words that brought her back to the moment. Guilt and fear were just waiting to punch their way out of the paper bag of a marital spat that they were dancing around, but standing in front of the Emerald waiting for Frankie Calabro to show his face was too much for her. She felt exposed out on that sidewalk. Though there was no one else on the street, she felt the eyes and ears of her past all over her. She surrendered for the sake of her sanity.

"Let's just go get Christina and go home, Paul. It's not even three o'clock and it's already been a long day."

"What are you fucking kidding here, Tina? You ride in here on a broomstick and start making demands. You've already embarrassed the shit out of me in there and now you want me to follow you home like a bad puppy? You go home. I've got some business with Dom."

"Business with Dom? What are you talking about, Paul? You haven't seen Dom in years, now you have *business* with him! You never had business with Dom, what kind of *business* could you have all of a sudden?"

What could Paul possibly want with Dom? Which Dom was he

even talking about - Dom the bookie or Dom the guy who Frankie beat and robbed.

Her life was suddenly spinning out of control. Until that phone rang last night, she was fine. Gina's call sent Paul running, right to the Emerald, right to that asshole Jerry Morano. Now she was the one running. Running from the one moment in her life that she thought was so far behind her that it could never catch her. But she was wrong. It wasn't behind her at all; she was running straight into it.

She wanted to cry, but tears would belie her fear and crack the mask of anger that she presented to Paul. She still hoped that this could still turn in her favor. Her hopes only lasted a second longer.

"Go home, Tina," Paul said flatly, and turned from her. "Go get *your* daughter and go home."

"Our daughter," she said. "*Our* daughter, Paul."

Her heart dropped in her chest. Paul had turned his back on her. There wasn't much more than a string of a lifeline left connecting her to her sanity.

He stopped and turned. His eyes were blank, not angry or tearful, just blank; waiting for the situation to give them life.

"Tell me something about Frankie Calabro, Tina. Tell me something I don't know. Tell me something that Jerry, or Gina, or Jimmy, or everyone else doesn't know. Tell me, why you felt the need to hunt me down looking for Christina, why my wife is suddenly so concerned about my coming down to the Emerald?" His eyes began to fill with bile. "Tell me why Gina really came by last night in such a hurry? Why Jerry the fucking Dutchman thinks I would care more than anyone else if Frankie Calabro made an unexpected return?"

He believed them! He believed the cheap murmuring of other people over his years with her, his *life* with her. First Gina, and now Paul! He had no idea of the truth, he just lined up with them. Fuck the benefit of the doubt; he should have believed in her, he should have *known* the truth. She had been protecting him from all of this, yet he cut her loose. Everything she depended on in her life now seemed like no more than a fistful of sand.

A feeling of complete isolation circled her and began to shrink, to push against her, just like the cheesy carnival ride that pressed you against the wall as it spun and dropped the floor out from under you. She closed her eyes and waited to die, but death never came. Instead, she found quiet. None of the screams of dread were waiting for her. Only quiet. The carnival ride was over before it even began. The knot in her chest was no more and her lungs filled with air. She didn't understand. Where had all the anxiety gone? Where was all the doubt and whispering panic, the mocking fear? It was gone. In its place was…acceptance. She had an unobstructed view of the dismantling of her life and she was calm in resignation. She was living out an unspoken prophecy mandated by her long-ago act, even though it wasn't the act that was being cast upon her by everyone around her. Her true deceit was mocking her, punishing her for her silence. She knew how to end it

"I did it."

The words came without pain or fear or anger. They came with relief and release. It was no confession, just a simple statement.

Paul's face didn't know what to do. His eyes went blank again and his lips swelled with a million painful words, yet not a sound escaped them. Without having to shame it out of her through a cascade of remorseful tears or make her scream it out in a rage of disgust, she just said it. She spoke the very thing he demanded her to say but that he never wanted to hear, and she just said it like it was nothing. Just like that.

The only thing he could muster was to repeat it back to her. Maybe he could see what he was supposed to feel in her reaction to the same words.

"You did it." Not a question, just the same statement.

Nothing. No tears, no scowl. Her face was almost

serene now, like she was glad to smash him with this after all these years of letting him play husband and lover…and father.

Paul saw no change in Tina, but she felt the change in herself. The words freed her to see clearly just how strong she was, and how weak Paul was. She saw his abandonment right before her eyes. She watched him fall right in line with Gina and Jerry. Gina was right, she was the "strong" one.

Paul wouldn't give her the satisfaction of a "how could you?". He wouldn't let her see how crushed he was, not with her standing there expecting him to forgive her. Standing like a fucking block of ice waiting for him to crumble at her feet. No. He would give back the same dispassion.

He began to stride back and forth before her; his arms unknowingly reaching up to rub his neck or clench in fists or splay out as if they just wanted to touch her.

"When did you become so *small*, Paul?" Tina said.

"Small? So I guess it would be *big* of me to let my fiancé fuck somebody else and just say 'Hey, that's okay. Just have her home by the wedding?'. Oh, not just somebody else, but the most fucked up psycho this neighborhood has ever seen! That would be real *big* of me."

"You're hearing but your not listening, Paul," she said.

"I'm listening, Tina. I'm listening really close to how much of an asshole you made out of me. Who else knows, Tee? How far does my reputation go? You know what? It doesn't matter. I'm going to right things when that prick shows up again. We'll see who the asshole is then. I'll straighten him right the fuck out, and then I'll deal with you."

"Oh, is that your 'business' with Dom. Now you're going to prove something to your friends? Is that why you came back here, to show Jimmy and Dom and Jerry what a *big* man you are?"

Paul's hands settled into fists and cocked themselves at his side. "I'm sorry. Does that upset you? Are you worried about Frankie now, Tina? Maybe you're glad he's coming back?" His pacing turned to stomping at this notion.

"Did you hear what I said, Paul? *I* did it. It was me."

His neck went purple and his eyes bulged with the pressure of fury.

"YOU? It was all YOU? Frankie was just an innocent swinging dick and you had to have him?"

The idea that Tina had pursued Frankie was one that Paul refused to acknowledge. It would have been too deep a cut, too brutal a betrayal. Every culture had its name for a man who knows his wife is fucking around yet does nothing about it. In his world, it was the worst of jokes to be another man's "husband by pussy". Paul could never be Frankie Calabro's "husband". A sick feeling swirled in his guts and he turned and crashed his fist into the door of the Emerald. The dull thud dropped to the doorstep with barely an echo.

"You too, huh Paul? That's all you could come away from this with – I was *fucking* Frankie Calabro? You are so damn stupid. You have no idea what this is even about, so you made it about the only thing you could understand – me, your dumb little girlfriend, fucking behind your back. You talk about my sister and how fucked up she is and how much you can't stand her, but here we are and you're just like her."

Paul's arms shot out toward Tina, finger pointing like spikes. "*I'm* like her, Tina? *I'm* like her? It's pretty clear that spreading legs is a family trait. But she's not as good a liar, hiding behind a wedding ring, hiding behind a daughter…"

He knew that this was the line in the sand that he could never step back from and he had just drawn it between himself and Tina. Her face finally showed some emotion, but he knew the price for making her feel his anger and loss might be too high. Tina was still his wife, still the only woman he had ever truly loved, but she had pushed him to this point. She was the one who betrayed their trust. He stood there at the line and was without words because the clenching of his guts told him that the next words would be the wrecking ball that would bash into a million little pieces whatever chance they had left.

Tina stood in the shock of Paul's last words. He had said what she wished was unspeakable. He brought Christina into the fight. That could only mean that somewhere inside he had doubts about her as well.

How could you, Paul? After everything I did for us. All this happened because of what I did for us. You're so fucking blinded by your own jealousy, so worried about a "reputation" that you don't even have that you can't hear what I'm saying. I did it, you asshole. Her thoughts became words without her even realizing. "I did it you stupid fuck. I took the money."

As deafened as he was by his own fury, his ears still sought out a whisper of hope through the din of the collapsing world between him and Tina. She said it again, only this time it was followed by more words that made no sense. *Took the money?* What did she say?

"What? What did you just say?"

"I took the money, you fucking asshole," Tina repeated. "This whole time you were busy pointing your finger at me, you had no idea what you were really pointing at. You and my sister and that other asshole Jerry, and God knows who else believed all this crap, were so quick to cast me as, what did you call me a 'leg spreader', that you couldn't even begin to wrap your little minds around the possibility that this had nothing to do with cheating or fucking or whatever else inhabits your little minds. I guess that's all women are capable of Paul. Just dumb little fuck toys. Is that it? Well I'm sorry to disappoint you, but I guess I'm not the woman you thought so little of."

"What are you talking about? You took what money?" Paul was beyond confused. His mind was floundering to absorb any of what was happening. He looked at the woman before him who resembled his wife, but she was somebody else. She was saying things that made no sense, that didn't fit with the person he was looking at, as if she was being dubbed like a cheap karate movie.

Tina felt an odd power in her face now; her lips

punched out her words and punctuated them with jabs.

"*I* took the money from Frankie Calabro. I followed him that night and stole the money from the back seat of his car while he went into his mother's house. Do you hear me now, Paul? I took Perillo's money from Frankie."

The words hit Paul hard enough to snap him out of his daze. His anger was gone and his confusion parted. *Tina took the money.* That was the statement that he was dealing with now. The tensed muscles of his body drooped and his hands went limp. His face slid slowly past his normal visage and surrendered into a bag of skin. She was right, the strange karate woman that had turned back into Tina. He could never have imagined what she was saying could be true. This wasn't her. This wasn't the girl he knew all this time. *You took the money? You took the money!* The dynamics of what came with this revelation hadn't become obvious to him yet, it was the simple idea that took up all his thoughts at the moment.

"What the fuck?"

It was the only thing he could think to say, but it addressed all the whys and hows and every other possible existing variable.

Paul's collapse back into himself softened Tina's resolve. Though she didn't owe him a response after his abandonment, she deserved the right to purge the last of her ghosts.

"I took it for the wedding." The relief that she had been granted by her earlier admission retreated and let her anxiety back in. All of the original fear and guilt that accompanied her actions from that night emptied from her memory into her chest.

"Where is this coming from?" Paul asked. "You never told me that there were problems with the wedding. And if there were, stealing money from fucking Frankie Calabro...from *Perillo*...certainly wasn't the answer!"

Tears welled in her eyes as a press of old emotions pushed against the inside of her head. The more powerful ones clustered themselves into resentment and ganged up on her. "What was the answer then Paul? Where was the money for the wedding going to come from?"

"You told me your father was paying for the wedding," Paul said.

"And I told him you were paying for it."

"Why would you do that?" His face was vacillating with emotions.

Why? It was the million dollar question she had been grappling with since the night she took the money. Paul was right; Frankie Calabro had no respect for anyone or anything. He was feral and fearless and took what he wanted when he wanted it. He had to have known what would happen if he robbed Perillo's money, yet he didn't care. It was different for her. She knew fear and guilt, but once Frankie took the money, she didn't see it as Perillo's anymore. She saw it as Frankie's, and stealing from him was almost like justice. Frankie stole because he plainly had to. He was obeying his nature. Tina took the money because she *needed* it. There was honor to her thievery.

"Because neither one of you could give me the wedding I wanted," she said bluntly. "In spite of your obvious lack of trust, I fully expected that to be my only wedding day and I wanted what I deserved as a bride. That was my day, Paul. My 'once in a lifetime' moment."

Paul deflated like a wobbly punching bag that had just been stabbed.

"You know, my grandmother always told me that the only real way to get what you want is to get it yourself. I've always secretly hoped she was wrong, but you proved her right today, Paul. You had no faith in me beyond what you saw with your dick. Men are such disappointments. *They can be loved and respected, but never trusted,* Nona told me. *They can be fathers and husbands, but they will always be boys.*"

"You talk about trust, but you never even gave me a chance. You could have come to me. We could have figured something out, Tina, but it's a little too late now."

"No, Paul. 'Figuring something out' is the same as doing nothing to you. I 'figured something out' on my own. I took that money, Paul, because I knew you couldn't."

"When did you become so hard, Tina?" he asked with no small amount of disillusionment. "Well, I guess the torch *has* been passed, huh? You're 'Head Witch' now aren't you?" He paced in a tight circle, his face crunching as if in the grip of a giant invisible fist, squeezing and releasing his head.

"Do you understand what you've said to me? I mean *really* understand? Old Man Perillo, Tina!" He paused as another thought sliced its way into his mind. "Does Calabro know about this too?" His hands went back up to his head in a gesture that could only be viewed as an attempt to stop it from popping off of his shoulders. "SHIT!"

"And there it is, Paul. Our marriage is dying at your feet and you're still worrying about what other people will say or do. Out of everything I just said to you, the only thing you can focus on is your own ass. You're trapped in the mentality of this neighborhood; still afraid of the same people you were afraid of when you were a teenager."

Paul spun away from Tina in a whirl of frustration and anger. He needed to clear her from his eyes, to gain a new perspective, but all he found was another vision to rend his mind. Standing in the doorway of Jimmy B.'s Emerald Bar was Dom Silvieri.

"I heard something slam against the door," Dom said. "I thought you might need some help out here."

Dom looked past Paul at Tina. She was standing as defiant as a weed growing up through a crack in the sidewalk. *Hell has no fury, huh? Hell ain't never seen anything like this girl.*

"You know, that piece of shit Calabro ain't worth all this," he said, moving his eyes to Paul. "You got too much to lose, Paulie. Let it go." He looked back at Tina, who met his eyes with a fearlessness usually reserved for men, then turned, pulled open the door and disappeared back into the Emerald.

Paul was drained. Drained of anger, drained of fear, and drained of confusion. He was more than a model of defeat; he was an empty soul sack. He turned back to his wife and opened his eyes like the mouths of baby birds waiting to be fed. He needed her to fill him back up, and he didn't care how much of himself would be lost. She was in charge now.

Prima Strega.

§

The inside of the church was quiet and more somber than in the heyday of the early Seventies when the old Bronx neighborhood that it served was more vibrant. The adjacent parochial school that bore its name had been closed a few years before by the Archdiocese after years of declining enrollment, a victim of the changing neighborhood. Few of the original parish families still attended mass each week. Even the once jam-packed Midnight Mass on Christmas Eve had been abandoned due to lack of interest. The overflow of youth that once ran in the streets of the neighborhood like rabbits had all grown and left their old homes for places of their own. Some moved to other parts of The Bronx, while some left the tired borough entirely for the illusory promise of the suburbs. Only the old stalwarts: the few remaining widows and eternal mourners, made regular showings in the empty pews. They came to pray for the souls of their miserable departed husbands and their errant children. On this day, a solitary woman knelt in the first pew, praying silently as she waited for the Pastor.

The old priest emerged from the sacristy, passed in front of the altar, kneeling and crossing himself as he did so, and came to sit in the bench with the woman. She finished her prayer and slid back into the pew.

"I have seen to everything," he said to the woman. "Pietro will personally meet your son and escort him to Mr.

Ruggierio."

"Thank you, Father," she replied, grasping his hand as she did. He moved to leave the pew and she kissed his hand as he stood. Her face was calm and resolute. She met his eyes with hers. Her cheeks were dry and her eyes were clear. "Thank you."

He nodded and made his way back to the room behind the altar. Once back in the privacy of the sacristy, he dared to think what he couldn't in the presence of the mourning woman. *She has shed many tears over her son. Too many. But now there are none left. May God help me, but this boy was lost from the day he was born.*

The sudden entrance of another man pulled him from his thoughts. It was Pietro, the rectory assistant. Pietro was an older man than the pastor, but he moved with an agility that defied his years. He had been at the parish since before the priest himself had even arrived. He was essentially an errand boy for the church. He tended to what was once a group of four priests at the parish, but now there was only the Pastor.

"I made the arrangements as you asked, Father. I will pick up the body at the airport and drive it back to the funeral parlor. Mr. Ruggierio has made all the calls to the police in Chicago." Pietro dropped his voice to be sure it didn't carry from the room. "He told me it may have to be a closed casket because of the boy's head. Gunshots, Father."

The priest just nodded to the man. Thinking again about Mrs. Calabro's dry eyes, he lowered his head in understanding.

Lost from the day he was born.

BOAR'S HEAD

He sat alone at the far end of the bar, nervously shifting about on the stool. His arms rested hard against the wooden edge of the bar top, his hands mindlessly tugging at each other as if trying to pull the fingers loose of their knuckles. He slouched into himself so far that his chin seemed to disappear into his chest, yet he would shoot up stiff-backed, neck craning and eyes peering out from the shadows of his brow whenever a shape passed the long window of the the Emerald Bar. He seemed to wait for the shadows to enter through the heavy door and turn into someone he was expecting. When no one entered, he would return to an impossibly deeper slouch.

His eyes bounced frantically back and forth from the old neon beer clock on the back wall to his wristwatch. "Where are they? Where the hell are they?" he mumbled.

"Hey Jimmy, anybody call?" he called out loudly.

Jimmy B. was at the opposite end of the bar on this slow fall evening, talking with a lone girl - the younger sister of one of Jimmy's longtime buddies. She was home on a long weekend from her upstate college, and, like many of the others who came home for visits from wherever they had moved on to, liked to stop in and talk with Jimmy. To most of the kids from the neighborhood, Jimmy Burke was as much a member of their family as any other. Many of the girls growing up around Jimmy had long unresolved crushes on him, and now – as young women - would like to resolve them. The reasons for her visit that night weren't even clear to her, but a visit with Jimmy was always good for feeling like you never left. Jimmy was leaning in close on one elbow, talking and smiling with the girl when the beckon came from the man at the other end.

"Hey Jimmy, anybody call," came the shout again.

He didn't respond nor miss a beat in his conversation, though he clearly heard the young man call. Jimmy could be deep in a conversation or busy tending other patrons, yet his bartender's ear caught every call, from loud shouts for beer to slight nods for another shot. Barroom etiquette can seem harsh to novices, but it is as valid as knowing your salad fork from your cake fork. Rudeness can cut through a noisy bar like a knife and Jimmy felt the loud call slice the air.

"Hey Jimmy! Jimmy! Anybody call?"

This time Jimmy mouthed the words, "Excuse me for one minute," to the girl as he turned to the now desperately peering man at the other end. He knew him. He knew him better than he may have wanted to. Jimmy was always fair in his treatment of the younger kids of the neighborhood, even when he didn't particularly care for some of them. This one he may have cared for the least, but in a way felt for the most. The young man twisted nervously on his stool as Jimmy approached.

"I'm sorry Jimmy, but tonight..."

Jimmy cut him short with a raised finger and a calm voice. "Alby, listen to me. What makes you think anybody is coming?"

He already knew what the call was about. The whole sad sequence of watching the door and pestering Jimmy had begun earlier in the evening. The anxious man had been twisting on his barstool for more than three hours. He insisted to Jimmy that there was to be a reunion of sorts at the Emerald tonight, a reunion that Jimmy knew was not going to take place. He had humored the persistent man for a while, but his patience was starting to wear thin.

"No one said anything to me. I haven't even seen Pete or Phil in here since last year. I saw Sean down on the Avenue the other day with his wife. We spoke for a half-hour and he didn't mention anything either. If they were coming here tonight don't you think they would have said something to me?"

"Yeah, but Jimmy..."

"No Alby. No buts," Jimmy spoke softly. "Give it another half-hour and then go on home and get some sleep."

"But Jimmy, it's not about me. It's for Tiv."

Alby's face was earnest as he invoked Tiv's name. He just couldn't understand how they hadn't come.

Jimmy looked down. He knew what was eating this guy up and he spoke to him in the soft tones of understanding - something only the true bartenders of the world can muster in the faces of failure worn by those who seek solace in the smoky barroom churches.

"All right. All right, Alby. Sit here for as long as you like, just don't keep asking me about the phone, and if nobody shows soon, please do yourself a favor and head on home. Okay, buddy?"

Jimmy's big hand reached out and curled around the back of the young man's neck, rubbing it gently. Jimmy turned to the trophy shelf, pulled down the bottle of Green label Jack and poured two shots.

"Here you go kid. For Tiv."

Alby's glassy eyes looked up at Jimmy as they downed the shots.

"They'll come Jimmy. You'll see. They won't forget what today is. They'll come for Tiv." His face gained an opaque confidence and he nodded his odd head in reinforcing punctuation.

"Right," Jimmy said solemnly, "They're coming. For

Tiv."

At Jimmy's utterance of Tiv's name Alby's face went flat as the air of his hopeful certainty rushed out of its balloon. His head sunk back to its resting-place in his neck.

Jimmy returned to the young girl at the end of the bar, stopping momentarily to pour two draughts for the Mangialardi brothers. Thursday was their designated night out together and that always meant a beer - or more - at Jimmy B.s'.

"Sorry about that," he apologized as he resumed his conversation.

"What's his problem," she asked, not attempting to mask her obvious distaste for the man at the other end of the bar. She was yet another among the majority group of young locals who grew up with Alby and weren't particularly fond of him.

"He's all right. He's just still hung up on this Tivoli thing," Jimmy said quietly.

"It's a year already, he should just get a life!" Her harsh words bore no real malice, they were more of a reflection of the even crueler pity that most held for Alby. "I don't understand why he kept hanging around with Johnny anyway. Johnny treated him like a dog. Worse than a dog. Since the first day that kid showed up in St. Dominic's, back in fifth grade, Johnny got on his case and never got off. Johnny was the one that nick-named him 'Boar's Head', you know, because he looked like the sign on the meat truck – the big head with that greasy black hair all pulled back. You could tell he just hated that name, but that made Johnny use it even more."

She shook her head in a manner that only the streets of the Bronx can cultivate. It was a gesture that carried more meaning than words could describe. This time it conveyed sad irony.

"I remember one time, when we were all around twelve or thirteen, a bunch of us were hanging around by the park, and all the boys were bragging about all the hair they had

…you know, down there," her head again gesturing, this time being used as a subtle pointing device. She smiled shyly, feeling a little foolish in front of the man for whom she was trying to seem like a grown woman, but she continued, her face still slightly flushed.

Jimmy smiled wide at her girlish embarrassment.

"Well anyway, we're all laughing and they're all bragging and Johnny gets a hold of Alby and tells him to show everybody his. Now you could tell that Alby was already all covered with hair by this age. It was kinda gross, you know," she paused a moment to mimic a grossed-out face. "Now, I'm there, Laurie and Kelly are there. So, Alby gets all red and says 'No,' to Johnny. Well, Johnny was always the joker in the bunch, but he was never really mean, you know. He always stopped his kidding if he saw someone getting really upset about it. He would even goof on himself if it were worth a laugh. Well, this day he snapped. He grabbed Alby and yelled at him to show everybody his stuff. He was yelling, 'Come on, *Boar's Head*. Come on!' Well, Alby said, 'No,' again and Johnny went crazy. He started slapping him and saying all kinds of nasty stuff to him until Alby says, 'Okay.' So, as the poor kid is dropping his pants, Johnny knocks him over, pulls his pants all the way off and takes off with them. Alby was all naked from the waist down, standing there with no place to hide. He starts begging Johnny for his pants, just shamed to Hell, with all of us dying laughing. I felt bad for him, but I just couldn't help laughing."

She glanced guiltily down toward Alby to see if he may have overheard her recount the embarrassing tale. He sat still and shadowy in the dim light, almost indistinguishable as a person. He could just as easily been a bunch of rags dumped on the barstool.

"Yeah, I felt real bad for him that day," she said again softly, "But it was one of those things that was funny. Funny, but nasty. You laugh, but you're really glad that it wasn't you. Kids can be cruel, huh?"

Not just kids, honey. Not just kids, he thought to himself, trying not to look over at Alby. Growing up didn't seem to help him much either.

"What I don't understand is what Johnny was doing hanging around with Alby in the first place," she added.

"Yeah, that was a strange pair," Jimmy said. "I don't get it myself, although there were times when Tiv would take care of Alby. There was the time he knocked around a couple of guys from Unionport who beat on Alby for something he had said to one of their girlfriends. Tiv brought Alby back here, propped him up in the Men's room and cleaned him up. Alby was pretty banged up, but Tiv sat him down and spent the whole night with him here."

"They were just so different," she said. "Johnny was so good-looking and fun. Alby is such a loser," she said quietly with another guilty glance toward Alby.

"He was one funny son of a bitch, that kid," said Jimmy with a hushed laugh. "One time, on a hot night, when my old jalopy air conditioner there had conked out, I had the door wide open and most people were hanging out front. Well, Tiv pulled up in this old junkbox convertible. He got out and put on this show about 'accidentally' locking the keys in the car. Now, I know he's up to something because on a hot, muggy night, he's in a ragtop with the top up, windows up and doors locked. Well, he acted real nonchalant about it and came inside for a couple of beers. Mind you, I watched this whole setup from the bar window, so I'm waiting for the finale. I think he knew I was on to him, because he finished up, winked at me and started telling everybody - inside and out - that he was leaving. I watched him as he headed for the car - cool as a cucumber - and put on another little show about the keys being locked inside the car. When he was sure he had everyone's attention as they laughed at his little predicament, he shrugged his shoulders, got behind the car a few steps, ran up the trunk and took a flying leap at the ragtop. There he went: up the trunk, feet first right through the top, and landed right in the driver's seat. Without missing a beat, as half of the idiots stood there with their mouths in mid 'oh, shits', he started the car and drove away with a quick toot from the old horn. The laughter was so loud that I was surprised no one called the cops. It was just the thing to take the edge off of a hot night. People were talking and laughing about that one for a long time after. Later, I found out that he had slit the top all the way through just before he came by." Jimmy laughed a little, then quieted down and shook his head sadly. "It was a real waste when he died. He was a little wild, but he was a good kid."

§

John Tivoli was a spirited kid. He was the only child of Angela and John Tivoli Sr. His father was a union electrician, and his mother was a typical housewife, busy making her side-street house the pride of Fillmore Street. Throughout his pre-teen years, Johnny was present with his mother every Sunday at the 10:15 Mass, his neatly pressed clothes trying vainly to keep him from twisting and twitching on the hard wooden pews. He barely managed to escape his mother's 'volunteering' him for altar service, and at the end of each Mass, along with all the other freshly unfettered angels, he took off down the church steps almost before the Priest could utter, "Go in peace", to join in an impromptu game of stickball.

As innocently wild as he was, Johnny was a charming kid. A rare combination of good looks, brains and charm that made him the most popular among his classmates and teachers, yet he never held himself over his peers. He was a likable and comfortably approachable boy. This was probably what led young Albert Cozean to cling to Johnny from the first day he walked into his new class at St.Dominic's.

Johnny was a hero for Alby to idolize and he thought that hanging around such a kid might make him something more in the eyes of his new classmates. A short, greasy skinned and hairy kid, Albert Cozean didn't have many friends. He never knew his father and never asked about him. His mother moved them from another Bronx neighborhood into a small apartment in a dark building, across from the train yard where the subway cars spent their idle time. The bricks of the old building were a greasy brown, as if the passing trains spat on them before disappearing into the subway tunnel. The street always looked oily and wet, like it had just rained. Vacant lots and small commercial buildings surrounded the old house whose other occupants were an old woman - whom no one ever seemed to see - and an erratic flow of strange, faceless tenants in and out of the basement apartment. The gray street was like a border town at the fringe of the neighborhood. Alby seemed to quickly absorb the dreary characteristics of his new surroundings. No other kids lived on the lonely street, so young Alby spent most of his time alone.

Being a newcomer, he didn't fit in at school. Most of the kids were born in the surrounding neighborhood and their cliques were inherited from their parents. Alby's mother worked at night and didn't socialize with any of the other school mothers. The only contact she made with the locals was a brief glance-less nod if she bumped into anyone as she came and went from church every morning. She went to the small, but impressively ornate, church for morning masses every day. She never took Alby, not even on Sundays when she attended the earliest mass there was. She more than occasionally had a meeting at the school at the Principal's request. She would stand stone-faced and silent, nodding her head in conjunction with the Principal's recommendations for correcting Alby's school performance and behavior. Her eyes would burn fiercely into Alby as she glanced over at him during these sessions. He knew the walk home would be quick, dead silent and end with a beating from a wooden kitchen spoon. He learned to block out his mother's terse berating to herself about wasting time and money sending him to a private school. He suspected all along that this was done for some guilty reasons of her own, rather than for his good.

The only connection Alby made with the other kids in the neighborhood was in his association with young Johnny Tivoli. He could stand the embarrassing jokes and the cruel tricks because they included him. Even the feeling of being alone in the crowd that always followed Johnny around was all right because he was still in that crowd. He didn't mind not being picked for stickball games because he could still watch and give Johnny a high five when he crushed a Spaldeen right out of the schoolyard. There were even a few glorious days when he could just be there and not be joked about or ignored. He liked the looks he sometimes got from other kids when they saw him walking along with Johnny after school. As long as John Tivoli was around, Albert Cozean could be somebody. Even if he was just a clinging shadow, he was at least that much more than someone alone.

§

"Last year, after the funeral, all the guys came here for a little send off for Tiv. It was some turnout, there had to be better than fifty people, guys I hadn't seen in years. We toasted John with a shot and said our good-byes," Jimmy said quietly. "I really don't remember Alby being there, but I know he was. Sean went on and on about all the stuff the guys did together when they were young, all the innocent mischief they stirred up together. All the girls were crying themselves silly over whatever they had with him, or wanted to have." Jimmy paused for a moment as if he had just remembered something. "I never knew why you weren't here."

She didn't look up at Jimmy as he waited for her response. A quietly sad look had gripped her pleasant face.

"I couldn't," she began slowly; "I just couldn't come. I still feel horrible about it, but I just couldn't. I grew up with the guy, you know. I was just starting college and I didn't want to deal with it all. Sometimes you have to let go and leave things behind you. You have to move on." Her eyes pled for understanding. She knew how bad it sounded even as the words were leaving her lips.

"Sometimes, all you have is what's behind you." Jimmy said. "Just look down at the other end of the bar." Alby now sat impossibly still. His hands no longer twisted, his eyes no longer darted. He sat frozen in a memory of something long gone. "He's under the impression that there's supposed to be some kind of reunion here tonight in honor of Tiv."

"Is there?"

"Not that I know of." Jimmy found himself again shaking his head sadly. "I don't know if you knew this, but I was the one who got the word." He looked out the window as he went on, "I got the call from Joe Grady, a buddy of mine in the Fire Department. You know his sister, Karen?"

"Yeah, I know her real well," she answered mechanically, her face changing quickly to one of sympathetic anguish. "I didn't know that. Oh, my God." She gently rubbed the big hand on the bar in front of her. She looked up at him with wet eyes. "Jimmy B., everybody's big brother. Is there anybody you don't know?"

Jimmy smiled at her, weakly veiling the sadness his voice had taken on. "I hope not!" he said with his best boyish grin. The smile faded and he continued his story. "Anyway, I got the call from Joe. He tells me they just cut a kid out of a car that was wrapped around one of the steel beams under the Westchester El. He couldn't recognize the body, it was too banged up, but he was wearing one of my shirts, you know those tee shirts I give out on Super Bowl night."

He tugged at his own shirt mindlessly, and she nodded.

"When he told me what kind of car it was I knew it was Tiv."

"How could you tell from the car?" she asked.

Jimmy looked down the bar before he answered. "It was Alby's car. Tiv had stopped in here real quick that night looking for Alby. He needed a car for something, probably a girl. Well, as soon as Alby pulls up outside, Tiv is out the door and hassling Alby for the keys."

"Oh my God!" she whispered and sucked in a tight little breath. "You mean it was in Alby's car. Johnny died in Alby's car!"

"Ssshhh, keep that to yourself. The guy feels bad enough that his only friend is dead, never mind that it happened in his car. Anyway, Tiv was always bogarting Alby's car. He would always disappear with it and not come back. Alby would have to go to his house the next day and pick it up."

Jimmy went on, but his voice seemed to fade from her ears. She found herself feeling terrible for Alby. Her memories began to nudge at her insides. Maybe if some of us had been nicer to him, the rest of the kids would have come around. Her guilt about missing the funeral quietly gnawed at her. She never said anything to the Tivoli's or sent a Mass card. She was starting to feel like a shit. She looked over at Alby. Maybe she should say something to him? He seemed to need the condolences tonight. In her mind she began to see Alby as more of a grieving widow than a sad friend, but this widow was more of a battered spouse than a lover in mourning.

She didn't know what to say, but she would say something. She would make it right. She would be saying she was sorry for more than his loss, she would be making up for all those years. What she didn't know was how tender the bruises of a lifetime still were.

"If you'll excuse me, I need a trip to the men's room. I'll be right back."

Jimmy's voice came back to her and she snapped back to their conversation. Jimmy was smiling again. She nodded her assurance that she would be here when he returned. She watched as Jimmy walked away and disappeared behind the swinging door of the Men's room, giving her the moment she needed. She balled up her nerve, stood up from the stool and began the long journey down the bar. She would set things right before Jimmy returned.

Alby no longer looked over at the beer clock. He came to accept the fact that no one was coming. He was passed wondering how they couldn't show up, and he was into the why. Matt, Pete, even Phil maybe … but Sean. How could Sean not show?

Sean Murphy and John Tivoli were as close as two friends could be. They lived a few houses apart, and their parents were good friends. The boys played together as toddlers, were in the same class together all through parochial school, and even attended the same high school. They shared laughter and dreams together, and when the time came for one of them to marry, the best man was a done deal. When Sean announced his engagement one night at the Emerald, the celebration lasted all night. Tiv beamed with pride for his friend, but that light never reached Alby. Sean' fiancé's distaste for Alby quickly extinguished any possible invitation to the wedding. Alby barely made it to the closed-door bachelor party at the Emerald, but the wedding was off limits. The Emerald was closed the night of the wedding; Jimmy B., along with most all of the patrons, was in attendance.

Alone again, Alby spent that night in his car, driving to no particular place. They were all assholes, he thought. All of them, even Tiv, he thought for a fleeting moment before Alby decided that Tiv had no choice but to go, being a neighbor and all. Sean could never know that what was to be a sweet memory for him would be such a bitter one for Alby.

On this night, Alby thought again how much he didn't need those assholes. The one's who didn't really care about

Tiv. He only meant something to them when he was around. Now they had to be something by themselves; they couldn't hang on to Tiv like leeches - hide in his shadow, be known as one of Tiv's friends. They were all full of shit as they cried and said how much they would miss him, how much he meant to them. Even Sean - the so-called best friend - didn't show. Alby thought about how Sean was the only one not to cry at the funeral. He was probably glad that Tiv was gone; now everybody would treat him like Tiv. He would inherit all the friends, but he would never be another Tiv. Not even close. Alby scowled as he thought about Sean, but the tears he thought were never shed did indeed pour down Sean' face - harder and longer than anyone else's did. The only person there to catch them fall was his wife. She saw the loss that Alby felt only he had suffered. Alby and Sean were woven together by memories they shared apart.

Alby sat alone again with his singular loss and hated all the others. In a way he was glad; he didn't want to share his grief. It was his. The one thing that was truly his and that no one else could take away. It was him and Tiv locked together forever, finally.

Just Alby and Tiv.

She trembled slightly as she got near Alby. He seemed lost in thought and didn't notice her approach. She still wasn't sure what she would say. Poor guy, she thought as she could now see him clearer. He really was a mess, all slumped over and buried under a mass of wrinkled clothes. Her years of dislike for him surfaced, but pity held them at bay. She would make him feel better and it would in turn make her feel better. She was close enough to be heard, so she pulled herself together and began softly.

"Alby." She waited as he turned toward her, startled out of his thoughts. His eyes were scary and she already wondered if she had done the right thing by coming over to him. Too late, she went on. "Alby, I just wanted to say how sorry I was when I heard about Johnny, I know you guys were friends..."

Alby cut her off, "You don't know anything. Just leave me alone!" He turned away from her and slumped back down into himself.

She was taken aback by his reaction and stood silent for a second - embarrassed, but determined to go on. "Come on, Alby. It was rough on all of us when he died, you especially, I know. He was a great guy and we're all going to miss him."

Alby turned toward her with a steaming fury. "You keep saying, 'I know', like you know something! You don't know anything. Nothing. Nothing about me, nothing about Tiv. I know something. I know that all these years you and the rest of them treated me like dirt. The only one who was my friend was Tiv. When none of you were around to push him, he treated me like a friend. It was only bad when all of you were around and you wanted a show. You wanted to see him make a jerk out of me. Alby the Jerk! No one really cared about Tiv, only what they could get out of him by being around him. Look around; see all the people who cared. They're not here. They couldn't give up one night to remember Tiv. Not ONE night!"

Alby's eyes shifted between fire and tears as he spoke. His face twisted with his anger and his hands clenched. She was sorry she had unleashed the tempest. As Alby's words sliced into her, she shrank down inside herself and cringed. With his last word he slammed his fist against the bar, stood up from the stool and silently pulled some money out of his pocket and placed it on the bar.

Without another glance at her, he passed out of the Emerald Bar. The old door marked his exit with a bellow of air that almost sounded like a gulp, as if the dark night had just swallowed him whole.

She stood trembling anew at what her meddling had wrought and felt worse than she had in the moments that led up to it. She walked quietly back to her seat at the end of the bar and amid silent tears she added one more regret to her memories of John Tivoli.

Jimmy came out of the bathroom and noticed that Alby was gone. He stopped where the nervous man had been sitting, removed his empty beer glass and wiped the bar with a towel. Poor bastard, he thought of Alby. He glanced up the bar at the young girl. She had shifted in her seat and was looking out the long bar window. The Mangialardi brothers were still in a huddle, talking quietly about who knows what, and for the first time that night, Jimmy B. noticed that the Emerald was quiet. He didn't usually give it much thought as he spent so much time in the place he could hardly tell one night or one crowd apart, yet tonight he could feel the quiet. Somehow, in the few short minutes that he was away, the room had changed.

For once, Alby's presence, or his absence, was significant.

§

The car turned onto the quiet side-street that ran through a small corner of the cemetery. St. Raymond's Cemetery was one of the largest Catholic cemeteries within the city limits, and because of its proximity to the Bruckner Expressway and Tremont Avenue, its myriad shadows and hiding places made it a very attractive place for hi-jinx or low crime

The unnamed street - part of a long ago deal between the city and St. Raymond's Church involving expansion of the cemetery and passage for the people of the surrounding neighborhood boxed in by it - cut off a small piece of the cemetery from the rest. It was a dark street, a little wider than normal, with no curbs or sidewalks. The grass of the cemetery crept under the tall wrought iron fence that surrounded it and met the cracking asphalt of the street like a gray-black surf clinging to a green beach. The single street lamp cast a dim light and quickened the long shadows of the fence upon the well-kept grass.

The car crept slowly rolled to a stop, almost into the

fence of the smaller part of the cemetery, yet still within the pale circle of light shed by the street lamp. A few seconds passed before the door opened and a lone figure stepped out. He carelessly climbed upon the hood of the car and hoisted himself onto the old fence, catching his coat on one of the iron spikes as he shakily made his way over the top. He hung limply on the inside of the fence, dangling by the coat arm until it ripped with a loud shredding noise, sending him flopping to the ground like a bundle of rags. Again, a few seconds passed before the man-bundle moved. He stood slowly, and without needing a glance around to determine his surroundings, headed steadily for his destination. He knew where he was; he had been here many times before, gates opened or gates locked.

In the first weeks after Tiv's death, Alby came to the cemetery everyday. He never spoke. He just came and sat on the ground, sometimes perfectly still, and others nervously twisting and tugging at himself. He never visited the grave if anyone else was there. He would wait outside on the street until they were gone; before he went to Tiv. He had taken to scaling the old fence at night so he could sit undisturbed by any other.

This night he came again, but he didn't think he would be alone. This was to have been the first time he would ask others to join him. He would let Kevin, Anthony and even Sean intrude on his private mourning because this was a different night. It was to be a night to honor Tiv. Alby was ready to let them join him in his tribute, only they didn't show up. None of them. They were all too busy with their little lives that they didn't have time for Alby, only it wasn't about Alby, it was about Tiv. He remembered the night in the bar - one year ago this night - that he said they should all get together every year on the anniversary of Tiv's funeral and toast him. The man who had been a friend to all of them. All of them; yet only Alby showed up.

What Alby didn't remember was how he really wasn't even a face in the crowd that night. He sat alone at the end of the bar watching the others as they cried, laughed, remembered and eulogized John Tivoli. Alby was no longer part of the crowd just because he was around them. That fringe benefit died with Tiv. The others had no concern for the clinging Alby. They toasted their friend without even noticing the sad outsider at the other end of the bar. Alby felt it that night, the sense of being beyond the fringe, outside the circle, but he didn't know any other way to be. That was always his place, and he knew it. Somehow he just hoped they had heard him when he offered up his salute to Tiv. In their semi-drunken dolor, one or more of them may have even joined Alby in a raised glass for their fallen brother, but it wasn't anything anyone remembered.

Except Alby.

A night about Tiv. Not the Tiv that was cruel, but the Tiv that was a friend who looked out for poor Alby. Not the Tiv that put on a show when others were around, but the Tiv that put his arm around Alby's shoulder or laughed with him, not at him. This was to be the night when all the others would see that Alby and Tiv were buddies, best friends. Alby would tell them all about the times he and Tiv cruised for girls and the times they sat for hours and talked. He would tell them all about him and Tiv, and then they would see that Alby was okay. He wasn't just some asshole. He could be everybody's friend.

Just like Tiv.

Alby looked up at the light gray stone that marked the head of John Tivoli's grave. It looked as if it were just set, its surface yet unweathered by the cemetery air. The letters and words on it meant nothing to him. The true epitaph was written on Alby's face. No chisel could have carved deeper lines or said more than the agony forever etched on his face. His dreary eyes poured forth grief and his formless mouth spoke unheard laments. The weight of his thoughts pulled his head down toward the beckoning ground.

As he sat, sinking slowly into the soft ground, he began

to speak. The reunion may not have been, but his tribute would go on.

"I'm here Tiv," he began softly. "It's been a year already."

His voice wavered as if he didn't want to disturb anyone else or let anyone hear him.

"I really miss you. I was just down at Jimmy B.'s. We went over there after the funeral last year…".

He paused at this memory for a moment, then began again, "I've been thinking a lot about us, you know. How we're real good friends and all, and how we know each other so long. You know, you are the person I know the longest. I know you know a lot of people, but for me, you're my oldest friend…, maybe my only friend."

Memories flooded over him as he thought about his life with Tiv. Loss and anger wrestled inside him each trying to win control over the wretched young man. He paused again as his words took shape in his head.

"We are friends, right Tiv? I mean even after all the things you did to me, all the lousy things you did for laughs, we are still friends, right? Tiv? You know I never got mad at you for that stuff. Not even the *Boar's Head* thing. I know it was just because of all the others that you did it. They wanted somebody to laugh at. It wasn't your idea."

Anger slowly shifted the tides in Alby's heart.

"That was it, right. I mean a friend wouldn't just do that, would they? Tiv? You know I planned a reunion tonight, kind of like a tribute to you, and you know what. Nobody came. Not even Sean. No, he must have been too busy. Why else would he just not show up? Why else would your so-called 'best friend' not show up? He was around for everything else. He always seemed to be around to make you do stuff with him when we had something else planned. He didn't care about that. He dragged you into his wedding just to have you around. He couldn't even do that by himself. But, you know what? You never even thought twice about leaving me behind, did you? I mean, I was always good when no one else was around, or if you needed some money. You did that to me a lot, you know? Left me behind for somebody else. But, what happened? Where are all these other people now? None of them showed up tonight. I know they knew about it. I told them all after the funeral. They all knew, but they didn't show. Why do you think that is Tiv? Why wouldn't anyone show up for your tribute."

Alby's long hidden anger began to shatter his careful memories like pieces of glass. His eyes tightened and his face pulled back.

"Maybe you're just not the hero I wanted you to be? Maybe I wasted all these years hanging around with a loser? Maybe it wasn't me everybody didn't like, huh? Maybe it was you! Maybe that's why you did all those things to me, made me look stupid in front of everyone? I could have been the one with all the friends, all the girls. I should have pushed you around, took your things and laughed behind your back."

Alby's fury poured out so fast tears began to stream down his twisting face, and he began pounding the ground with his fists. His thoughts raced screaming through his head.

"You took everything you wanted without even a 'Thanks Alby'. You took money from me and never paid me back. You took my car..."

Alby wasn't ready to face this last epiphany and as his thoughts crashed against his guilt, he collapsed onto the ground.

He sobbed gently as he lay upon the grave. His mind slowly gathered itself from the void into which it stared and chose survival. Hard loss replaced the anger that had invaded his heart.

"I'm sorry, Tiv. I didn't mean any of that. I just don't understand things, you know. I don't want to understand them. I'm kind of all alone now, you see. Before, I had you, even when you left me behind I still had you. I just don't know what to do anymore."

Alby sat back on his legs, touched the ground in front of him and silently forgave Tiv. He forgave him for all the cruelty and the magnified loneliness. Like a battered wife forgiving her abusive spouse, he gathered up all the excuses he had provided for Tiv's actions and carefully placed them back where they would protect his memories. Tiv was his friend, no matter what anyone else said. They just didn't know him the way Alby did.

Being alone was hard, but being alone without memories was too much to bear.

§

"Thanks, Tony," Jimmy said softly to the man bedside him as he grasped the chain and lock on the cemetery gate. "I'll just be a minute. Let me talk to him and maybe get him to go home."

"Alright Jimmy, but try and make it quick. I don't want to get any flack from the Church about this, you know. We're supposed to be keeping people out of here, not letting them in." Officer Anthony Schulman, another of Jimmy Burke's long line of friends and acquaintances, removed the lock from the tall black iron gate. St. Raymond's Church had given a set of keys to the Forty Seventh Precinct to give patrolmen access for dealing with vandalism in the old cemetery.

Jimmy B. headed for Tivoli's grave. He had been there for the burial and he knew where it was. It was only a moment before he saw Alby on the ground ahead of him - the same shapeless mass that had been on a stool in his bar earlier that night.

Jimmy reached out his hand and gently clasped Alby's shoulder. There didn't seem to be much under the mess of cloth that covered the man as Jimmy's hand squeezed deeper into the fabric. He had hoped his touch would reassure the man, but Alby didn't even seem to notice. He just kept looking down at the ground beneath him. It seems like two people died in that car wreck, Jimmy thought silently.

Jimmy squeezed Alby's shoulder a little tighter. "Come on, kid. Let's go on home."

It wasn't until Jimmy's hand touched Alby's shoulder, drawing him back into the cool night, that Alby quietly let go of his mourning. He gripped Jimmy with his lost eyes for a few moments, released him and turned to the grave once more. He stared down at it as he stood.

Without looking at Jimmy, he spoke. "He was my friend, you know. We really were friends."

Jimmy put his arm around the slumped shoulders of the ragged man. "I know, kid. I remember."

.